Jilly Cooper comes from Yorkshire but now lives in Gloucestershire with her family and an assortment of dogs and cats. Her journalism was a feature for many years of the *Sunday Times*, and more recently of the *Mail on Sunday*, and she has made many television appearances, including *What's My Line?* Her latest novel, RIVALS, was a number one bestseller.

Also by Jilly Cooper

RIVALS
RIDERS
EMILY
HARRIET
OCTAVIA
IMOGEN
PRUDENCE
CLASS
SUPER COOPER
LISA & CO.

and published by Corgi Books

Jilly Cooper

Bella

BELLA
A CORGI BOOK 0 552 10427 2

Originally published in Great Britain by
Arlington Books Ltd.

PRINTING HISTORY
Arlington edition published 1976
Corgi edition published 1977
Corgi edition reprinted 1978
Corgi edition reprinted 1979 (twice)
Corgi edition reprinted 1980 (three times)
Corgi edition reprinted 1981
Corgi edition reprinted 1983
Corgi edition reprinted 1984
Corgi edition reprinted 1985
Corgi edition reprinted 1986 (twice)
Corgi edition reprinted 1988
Corgi edition reissued 1989
Corgi edition reprinted 1989

This book is set in 10 on 10½pt Period

Corgi Books are published by Transworld Publishers Ltd., 61–63 Uxbridge Road, Ealing, London W5 5SA, in Australia by Transworld Publishers (Australia) Pty. Ltd., 15–23 Helles Avenue, Moorebank, NSW 2170, and in New Zealand by Transworld Publishers (N.Z.) Ltd., Cnr. Moselle and Waipareira Avenues, Henderson, Auckland.

Printed and bound in Great Britain by
Cox & Wyman Ltd., Reading, Berks.

To Laura
with love

AUTHOR'S NOTE

I have always wanted to write a novel about an actress and I started writing BELLA in 1969. However, at that time I wrote it as a *novella*, called it COLLISION and it was serialized in **19**. Only now am I able to fulfil my original wish and present the story as a full-length novel – BELLA.

Bella

CHAPTER ONE

BELLA read faster and faster until she came to the final page then, giving a howl of irritation, hurled the book across the room. Narrowly missing a row of bottles, it fell with a crash into the waste-paper basket.

'Best place for it!' she said furiously. 'How corny can you get?'

She escaped completely into every book she read, identifying closely with the characters. This time she was incensed because the heroine had slunk dutifully home to her boring husband instead of following her dashing lover up the Amazon.

She shivered and toyed with the idea of letting the water out and running more hot in, but she had done this four times already. Her hands were wrinkled and red from the dye of the book, and the sky that filled the bathroom window had deepened since she'd been in the bath from pale Wedgwood to deep indigo, so she knew it must be late.

She splashed cold water over her body, heaved herself out of the bath and stood, feeling dizzy, on the bath-mat. The bath was ringed with black like a football sweater, but the char would fix that in the morning.

Taking her wireless, she stepped over the debris of her clothes, picked up the second post which was lying in the hall, and wandered into the bedroom.

She turned up the music, danced and sang a few bars, then caught sight of herself in the mirror, hair hidden in a mauve bath-cap, body glowing red as a lobster.

The Great British Public would have a shock if they could see me now, she thought wryly.

She pulled off her bath-cap and examined herself more carefully. She was a big girl with a magnificent body and endless legs. Her mouth was wide and her large sleepy yellow eyes rocketed up at the corners. A mane of reddish-blonde hair spilled over her shoulders. The overall impression was of a sleek and beautiful racehorse at the peak of its condition.

She opened her letters. One was from a journalist who wanted to interview her, another an ex-boyfriend trying to come back and several forwarded by the B.B.C. from fans:

'Dear Miss Parkinson,' wrote one, in loopy handwriting, 'I hope you don't mind my writing. I know you must lead such a busy, glamorous life. I think it's marvellous the way there's never any breath of scandal attached to your name. Could you possibly send me a signed full-length photograph and some biographical details?'

Oh, God! thought Bella, feeling slightly sick, if only they all knew.

The last letter was practical. It was headed the Britannia Theatre, and was from the Director, Roger Field, who had written:

'Dear Bella,

If you're late again, I shall sack you. Can't you see how it unnerves the rest of the cast? Stop being so bloody selfish.

Love, Roger.'

Roger, Bella knew, would be as good as his word. She looked at the alarm clock by the bed and gave another howl of rage. It was twenty past six, and the curtain went up at seven-thirty. Dressing with fantastic speed, not even bothering to dry herself properly, she tore out of the flat and was fortunate to find a taxi almost at once.

The Britannia Theatre Company was one of the great theatrical successes of the decade. It specialized in Shakespeare and more modern classics and generally had three plays running on alternate nights and three in rehearsal. Bella had joined the company a year ago and had risen from walk-on parts to a small speaking part in *The Merchant of Venice*. She had recently had her first real break playing Desdemona in *Othello*. The critics had raved about her performance and the play had been running to capacity audiences for three nights a week.

Lying back gazing out of the taxi window at the trees of Hyde Park fanning out against a rust-coloured sky, Bella tried to keep calm. From now until her first entrance she would be in a nervous sweat, stage fright gripping her by the throat like an animal. She deliberately always cut it fine because it meant that she would be in such a hurry dressing and making up, she wouldn't have time to panic.

And yet, ironically, the only time when she felt really secure was when she was on stage, getting inside someone else's personality.

The taxi reached the theatre at five past seven.

'Evening, Tom,' said Bella nervously, scuttling past the man at the door.

He put down his evening paper and glanced at his watch. 'Just made it, Miss Parkinson. Here's a letter for you, and there're some more flowers in your room.'

Not bothering to glance at her letter, Bella bounded upstairs two steps at a time and fell into the dressing-room she shared with her best friend, Rosie Hassell, who played Bianca.

'Late again,' said Rosie, who was putting on eye make-up. 'Roger's been in once already, gnashing his teeth.'

Bella turned pale. 'Oh, God, I couldn't get a taxi,' she lied, throwing her fur coat on a chair and slipping into an overall.

'I think Freddie Dixon's after me,' said Rosie.

'You think that about everyone,' said Bella, slapping grease-paint on her face.

'I don't – and, anyway, I'm usually right. I know I am about Freddie.'

Freddie Dixon was the handsome actor playing Cassio. Both Bella and Rosie had fancied him and been slightly piqued because he'd shown no interest in either of them.

'You know the clinch we have in the fourth act?' said Rosie, pinning on snakey black ringlets to the back of her hair. 'Well, last night he absolutely crushed me to death, and all through the scene he couldn't keep his hands off me.'

'He's not meant to keep them off,' said Bella. 'I expect Roger told him to act more sexily.'

Rosie looked smug. 'That's all you know. Look, you've got more flowers from Master Henriques,' she added, pointing to a huge bunch of lilies of the valley arranged in a jam jar on Bella's dressing table.

'Oh, how lovely,' cried Bella, noticing them for the first time. 'I wonder what he's on about tonight.'

'Aren't you going to read his letter?' said Rosie.

Bella pencilled in her eyebrow. 'You can – since you're so nosey,' she said.

Rosie took the card out of its blue envelope.

' "Dear Bella," ' she read. 'That's a bit familiar. It was "Dear Miss Parkinson" last time. "Good Luck for tonight. I shall be watching you. Yours, Rupert Henriques." He must be crazy about you. That's the eighth time he's seen the play, isn't it?'

'Ninth,' said Bella.

'Must be getting sick of it by now,' said Rosie. 'Perhaps he's doing it for "O" levels.'

'Do you think he's that young?'

'Expect so – or a dirty old man. Nobody decent ever runs after actresses. They've usually got plenty of girls of their own.'

Bella fished a fly out of her bottle of foundation and had another look at the card. 'He's got nice writing though,' she said. 'And Chichester Terrace is quite an okay address.'

There was a knock on the door. It was Queenie, their dresser, come to help them on with their costumes. A dyed-in-the-wool cockney with orange hair and a cigarette permanently drooping from her scarlet lips, she chattered all the time about the 'great actresses' she'd dressed in the past. Bella, who was sick with nerves by this stage, was quite happy to let her ramble on.

'Five minutes, please! Five minutes, please!' It was the plaintive echoing voice of the callboy.

Bella looked at herself in the mirror, her smooth, young face belying the torrent of nerves bubbling inside her. Then she sat down on the faded velvet sofa with the broken leg in the corner of the room and waited, clasping her hands in her lap to stop them shaking.

'Beginners, please! Beginners, please!' The sad echoing voice passed her door again.

Rosie, who didn't come on until later, was doing the crossword. Bella took one more look round the dressing-room. Even with its bare floor and blacked-out windows, it seemed friendly and familiar compared with the strange brightly lit world she was about to enter.

'Good luck,' said Rosie, as she went out of the door. 'Give Freddie a big kiss.'

They stood waiting by the open door under a faded orange bulb – Brabantio, Cassio and herself. Wesley Barrington, who was playing Othello, stood by himself, a huge handsome Negro, six and a half feet tall, as nervous as a cat, pacing up and down, murmuring his lines like an imprecation.

The three of them left her. Help me to make it, she prayed.

Othello was speaking now in his beautiful measured voice: 'Most potent, grave and reverend signiors'

In a moment she would be on. Iago came to collect her.

'Come on, beauty,' he whispered. 'Keep your chin up.'

It had begun. She was on. Looking round the stage, beautiful, gentle, a little shy. 'I do, perceive here a divided duty,' she said slowly.

She was off, then on again, flirting a little with Cassio, and then Othello was on again. Here, where she found life a thousand times more real than in the real world, she had words to express her emotions.

But all too soon it was over. The appalling murder scene was ended and the play had spent its brief but all too vivid life.

And as she took her curtain calls, she had nearly reached the limits of her endurance. Three times Othello and Iago led her forward and the tears poured down her cheeks as the roars of applause increased.

'Well done,' said Wesley Barrington in his deep voice.

Bella smiled at him. She fancied him so much when they were acting, but now he was Wesley again, living in Ealing with a wife and three children.

Bella would now go out for a cheap dinner with Rosie and in the morning she would lie sluttishly in bed until lunchtime. She avoided the busy, glamorous world that her fans imagined she lived in. It was a question of conserving her energy for what was important.

In their dressing-room, however, she found Rosie in a fever of excitement. 'Freddie's asked me out.'

'I expect he wants to discuss the way you've been upstaging

him,' said Bella. She collapsed on to a chair and felt depression descending on her like dust on a polished table.

Not that she wanted Freddie to ask her out. She'd long ago decided his curly hair and neon smile weren't for her. But if he started up a serious affair with Rosie, there'd be no more cosy little dinners, no more Rosie and Bella, united and gossiping together against the rest of the cast. Still, it was nice for Rosie.

'Where's he taking you?'

'Somewhere cheap. He's amazingly mean. Do you think one ear-ring looks sexy?'

'No, silly. As though you'd lost the other one.'

There was a knock on the door. It was Tom, the doorman.

'There's a Mr. Henriques downstairs, Miss Parkinson. Wonders if he could come up and see you.'

'Oh,' said Bella, suddenly excited. 'What's he like?'

'Looks orl right,' said Tom, fingering a five pound note in his pocket.

'Not a schoolboy?'

Tom shook his head.

'Nor a dirty old man?'

'No, quite a reasonable sort of bloke. Bit of a nob really. Plum-in-the-marf voice and wearing a monkey suit.'

'Oh, go on, Bella,' said Rosie. 'He might be super.'

'All right,' said Bella. 'I can always tell him to go if he's ghastly.'

'Great!' said Rosie. 'I'll finish off my face in the loo.'

'No!' yelped Bella, suddenly nervous. 'You can't leave me.'

At that moment Queenie, the dresser, appeared at the door.

'You'd better get out of that dress before you spill make-up all over it,' she said to Bella.

Bella looked at herself in the mirror. Against the low-cut white nightgown, her tawny skin glowed like old ivory.

Let's knock Mr. Henriques for six, she thought.

'Can I keep it on for a bit, Queenie?' she asked.

'And I'm supposed to hang about until you've finished,' said Queenie sourly.

'Come on, you old harridan,' said Rosie, grabbing her arm and frog-marching her out of the room.

'You can have a swig of Freddie's whisky to cheer you up.'

Bella sprayed on some scent, then sprayed more round the

room, arranged her breasts to advantage in the white dress and, sitting down, began to brush her hair.

There was a knock on the door.

'Come in,' she said huskily in her best Tallulah Bankhead voice.

As she turned, smiling, her mouth dropped in amazement. For the man lounging in the doorway was absurdly romantic looking, with very pale delicate features, hollowed cheeks, dark burning eyes, and hair as black and shining as a raven's wing. He was thin and very elegant, and over his dinner jacket was slung a magnificent honey-coloured fur coat.

They stared at each other for a moment, then, smiling gently, he said: 'May I come in? I hope it's not a nuisance for you.'

He had an attractive voice, soft and drawling. 'My name's Rupert Henriques,' he added as an afterthought.

'Oh, please come in.' Bella stood up, flustered, and found that her eyes were almost on a level with his.

'You're tall,' he said in surprise. 'You look so small on the stage beside Othello.'

Embarrassed, Bella tipped a pile of clothes off the red velvet sofa.

'Sit down. Have a drink.' She got out a bottle of whisky and a couple of glasses. She was furious that her hand shook so much. She rattled the bottle against the glass and poured out far too large a drink.

'Hey, steady,' he said. 'I'm not much of a drinker.'

He filled the glass up to the top with water from the wash-basin.

'Do you mind if I smoke?'

She shook her head and was pleased to see his hand was shaking as much as hers when he lit his cigarette. He wasn't as cool as he looked.

As she sat down she knocked a jar of cold cream on to the floor. They both dived to retrieve it and nearly bumped their heads.

He looked at her and burst out laughing.

'I believe you're as nervous as I am,' he said. 'Aren't you used to entertaining strange men back-stage every night?'

Bella shook her head. 'I'm always frightened they might be disappointed when they meet me in the flesh.'

'Disappointed?' He looked her over incredulously. 'You must be joking.'

Bella was suddenly conscious of how low her dress was cut.

'The flowers are heavenly,' she said, blushing. 'How on earth did you manage to get such beautiful ones in winter?'

'Rifling my mother's conservatory.'

'Doesn't she mind?'

'Doesn't know. She's in India.' He smiled maliciously. 'I'm hoping an obliging tiger might gobble her up.'

Bella giggled. 'Don't you like her?'

'Not a lot. Do you get on with your parents?'

'They're dead,' said Bella flatly, and waited for the conventional expressions of sympathy. They didn't come.

'Lucky you,' said Rupert Henriques. 'I wish I were an orphan – all fun and no fear.'

He had a droll way of rattling off these remarks which made them quite inoffensive. All the same, she thought, he's a spoilt little boy. He could be quite relentless if he chose.

He picked up his drink. 'You were even better than usual tonight.'

'Don't you get bored seeing the same play night after night?'

He grinned. 'I'm glad it's not a Whitehall farce. You're the only reason I've been so many times.'

There was a knock on the door.

'Hell,' he said. 'Do we have to answer it?'

It was Queenie.

'I won't be a minute,' Bella said to her. 'I'm sorry,' she added to Rupert, 'I shall have to change.'

He drained his glass, got up and moved towards the door.

'I was wondering if you'd have dinner with me one evening next week,' he said.

It's Monday now, thought Bella. He can't be that keen if he can wait at least a week to see me!

'I'm very tied up,' she said, untruthfully.

'Tuesday?' he said.

'I'm working that night.'

'Wednesday then?'

She paused just long enough to get him worried, then smiled: 'All right, I'd like to.'

'I don't suppose you like opera.'

'I adore it,' lied Bella, determined to keep her end up.

'Great. There's a first night of Siegfried next Wednesday. I'll try and get tickets.'

As he left he said, 'I'm sorry I had to make your acquaintance in this rather gauche fashion, but I didn't know anyone who knew you, who could have introduced us, and the only other alternative would have been to have bought the theatre.'

It was only later that she discovered he was only half-joking. The Henriques family could have bought every theatre in London without batting an eyelid.

CHAPTER TWO

PROMPTLY at six-thirty on Wednesday he picked her up.

'You look gorgeous,' he said, walking round her.

'You don't look so bad yourself,' she said.

He was wearing a very dark green suit with a red silk shirt.

'You like it?' he said, pleased. 'My tailor only finished it on Monday; that's why I couldn't ask you out last week.'

An Aston Martin was waiting outside; music blasted out of the slot stereo; the heat was turned up overpoweringly.

Bella wound down her window surreptitiously as they drove off. She didn't want to be scarlet in the face before she started.

As they stopped at the traffic lights, Rupert turned and smiled at her. 'You shouldn't have made me wait so long to see you,' he said. 'I've been in such a state of anticipation I've been unbearable to everyone.'

Even in the thick of a first-night audience with the diamonds glittering like hoar frost, everyone turned to stare at them. Rupert seemed to know lots of people, but he merely nodded and didn't stop to chat.

The curtain hadn't been up for five minutes before Bella decided that Wagner wasn't really her. All those vast men and women screaming their guts out. She glanced at her programme and was appalled to see she was expected to sit through three acts of it.

Somehow she managed to endure the first act. It seemed so strange to be on the other side of the curtain.

'Is it all right? Are you enjoying yourself?' asked Rupert as he fought his way back to her side with drinks during the interval.

'Oh, it's great,' she lied enthusiastically.

Rupert looked dubious. 'Well, I don't know; they make a frightful row. Say as soon as you're bored and we'll leave.'

Two earnest-looking women with plaits round their heads turned to look at him in horror.

During the second act Rupert became increasingly restless, but cheered up when Brünhilde made her appearance.

'She looks just like my mother,' he whispered loudly to Bella, who gave a snort of laughter.

A fat woman in front turned round and shushed angrily. Rupert's shoulders shook. Bella gazed firmly in front of her but found she couldn't stop giggling.

'I say,' said Rupert a minute later, 'shall we go?'

'We can't,' said Bella horrified. 'Not in the middle of an act.'

'Will you be quiet,' hissed the fat woman.

'My wife feels faint,' Rupert said to her and, grabbing Bella by the hand, he dragged her along the row, tripping over everyone's feet.

Outside the theatre they looked at each other and burst into peals of laughter.

'Wasn't it awful?' he said. 'I wanted to impress you, taking you to a first night, but this really was the end.'

As they picked their way through Covent Garden's debris of cabbage leaves and rotten apples he took her hand. 'We'll have a nice dinner to make up for it.'

They dined in Soho; very expensively, Bella decided. Crimson velvet menus with gold tassels, and rose petals floating in the finger bowls. They sat side by side on a red velvet banquette, rather like being in the back row of the cinema.

'What do you want to eat?' Rupert asked her.

'Anything except herrings.'

He laughed. 'Why not herrings?'

Bella shivered. 'My mother forced me to eat them when I was young. I was locked in the dining-room for twelve hours once.'

Rupert looked appalled. 'But I've never had to eat anything I didn't like.'

'This is a nice place,' said Bella.

'It's a haunt of my father's,' said Rupert. 'He says it's the one place in London one never sees anyone one knows.'

'Rupert, darling!' A beautiful woman with wide-set violet eyes was standing by their table.

'Lavinia.' He stood up and kissed her. 'How was Jamaica?'

'Lovely. I can't think why I came home.'

'Have you met Bella Parkinson?'

'No, I haven't. How do you do?' She looked Bella over carefully. 'I've read all about your play, of course. Macbeth isn't it? I must come and see you.'

She turned back to Rupert and said, a little too casually, 'How's Lazlo?'

'In Buenos Aires.'

She looked relieved. 'That's why he hasn't rung. When's he coming back?'

'Next week sometime.'

'Well, give him my love and tell him to ring me before my sun-tan fades.' She drifted off to join her escort at the other end of the room.

'She's beautiful,' sighed Bella, admiring her beautifully shod feet. 'Who is she?'

'Some bird of Lazlo's.'

'Who's he?'

'My cousin.' He lowered his voice. 'Evidently Lazlo complained her bed was too small, so she went out to Harrods and bought one three times the size.'

'She's *mad* about him. Is he attractive?'

'Women think so. I know him too well. We work together.'

'What at?'

'Banking. We've got a bank in the City. But most of our business is tied up in South America. My father's chairman but Lazlo really runs it.'

'You look a bit Latin yourself.'

'My father's South American. My mother, alas, is pure English. She's coming home next Friday, worse luck. I'm hoping someone will hi-jack her plane. She keeps sending me postcards telling me not to forget to water the guides.'

Bella giggled. 'Who?'

'One of her interests along with the Blind, the Deaf, the Undernourished, and any other charity she can poke her nose into. Alas, there's no charity in her heart. Her life is spent sitting on committees and my father.' He looked at Bella. 'What were your parents like?'

Bella's palms went damp. 'My father was a librarian,' she

said quickly. 'But he died when I was a baby, so my mother had to take a job as a school mistress to support me. We were always terribly poor.'

Poor but respectable. She'd told the same lies so often that she'd almost come to believe them.

Their first course arrived – Mediterranean prawns and a great bowl of yellow mayonnaise. Bella gave a little moan of greed.

Later, when she was halfway through her duck, she suddenly looked up and saw that Rupert was staring at her, his food untouched.

'Bella.'

'Yes.'

'Will you have dinner with me tomorrow?'

'Of course,' she said. She didn't even stop to consider it. The one thing that could have spoilt her evening was the sense of being a failure, that he'd get to know her a little and then decide she was a bore.

Later, they went back to her flat for a drink and Bella drew back the curtains in the drawing-room to show Rupert the view. Half London glittered in front of them.

'Isn't it gorgeous?' said Bella ecstatically.

'Not a patch on you, and you've got the most beautiful hair in the world.' He picked up a strand. 'Just like Rapunzel.'

'Who's she?'

'The princess in the tower who let down her hair and the handsome prince climbed up and rescued her. You must have read it as a child?'

Bella looked bleak. 'My mother didn't approve of fairy stories.'

Rupert frowned and pulled her into his arms. 'The more I hear of your childhood the less I like it,' he said.

Then he kissed her very hard. After a minute he pulled her down on to the sofa and began fiddling with her zip.

'No,' she said, stiffening.

'Why not?' he muttered into her hair. 'Christ, Bella, I want you so much.'

Bella took a deep breath and burst into tears. One of her greatest acting accomplishments was that she could cry at will.

She had only to think of the poor unclaimed dogs at Battersea Dogs' Home, waiting and waiting for a master that never came, and tears would course down her cheeks.

'Oh, please don't,' she sobbed.

Rupert was on his knees beside her. 'Darling. Oh, I'm sorry. Please don't cry. I shouldn't have rushed things. I've behaved like a pig.'

She looked at him through her tears. 'You won't stop seeing me because I won't?'

He shook his head wryly. 'I couldn't if I tried now. I'm in too deep.'

After he'd gone she looked at herself in the mirror. 'You're a rotten bitch, Bella. God, you're in a muddle,' she said slowly.

She wanted men to want her, but once they tried to get involved she ran away, frightened they'd find out the truth.

CHAPTER THREE

RUPERT arrived next evening, his arms loaded with presents.

'I've decided you missed out on a proper childhood, so we're going to start now,' he said.

In the parcels were a huge teddy bear, a Dutch doll, a kaleidoscope, a solitaire board filled with coloured marbles, a complete set of Beatrix Potter and *The Wind in the Willows*.

Bella felt a great lump in her throat. 'Oh, darling, you shouldn't spend all your money on me.'

Rupert took her face in his hands. 'Sweetheart, listen. There's one thing you must get into your head; there are a hell of a lot of disadvantages about being a Henriques, but being short of bread isn't one of them.' He held out his hands. 'We've got buckets of it. My father's worth a fortune and, since Lazlo put a bomb under the bank, we're all worth a lot more. I've got a private income of well over £25,000.'

Bella's jaw dropped.

'That's what's so lovely about you, Bella. Anyone else would know about the Henriques millions. I've never worried about money in my life, and when I was twenty-one last month I inherited . . .'

'Twenty-one?' said Bella quickly. 'You said you were twenty-seven.'

He looked shame-faced. 'I did, didn't I? I knew you wouldn't be interested in me if you knew how young I was.'

'But I'm twenty-three,' wailed Bella. 'I'm cradle-snatching.'

'No you're not,' he snuggled against her. 'Anyway, I'm crazy about older women.'

From then on they were inseparable, seeing each other every night, touring the smart restaurants and getting themselves talked about.

As spring came, turning the parks gold and purple with crocuses, Bella found herself growing more and more fond of him. He was very easy to like, with his languid grace, sullen pent-up beauty, and his appalling flashes of malice that were never directed at her.

But he could be moody, this little boy who had always had everything he wanted in life. His thin face would darken and she could feel his longing for her like a volcano below the surface.

The eternal late nights were taking their toll of his health too. He had lost pounds and there were huge violet shadows beneath his eyes.

One May evening they were sitting on the sofa in her flat, when he said, 'Don't you mind that I never take you to parties and things?'

She shook her head. 'The only parties I like are for two people.'

Rupert turned her hand over and stared at the palm for a minute, then said, 'Why don't we get married?'

Panic swept over Bella. 'No!' she said nervously. 'At least, not yet.'

'Why not?'

'We come from different backgrounds. I've always been a have-not, you've always been a have. Your family would loathe me. I haven't any background.' She gave a slightly shaky laugh. 'When I talk about the past, I mean yesterday.'

'Rubbish,' Rupert said angrily. 'Don't be such a snob. I love you and that's all that matters.'

'I love you too.' Bella pleated the folds of her skirt.

'You're making things impossible for me,' said Rupert sulkily. 'You won't marry me; you won't sleep with me. I'm going out of my mind.'

He got up and strode up and down the room. He looked so ruffled and pink in the face, Bella suddenly had an hysterical desire to laugh.

'There's someone else,' he said, suddenly stopping in front of her.

'How could there be? I've seen no one but you for the last six months.'

'And before that?'

'Casual affairs.'

He caught her wrist so hard that she winced with pain.

'How casual? I don't believe you! You're as passionate as hell beneath the surface, Bella. One only has to see you playing Desdemona to realize that.'

Bella had gone white. She snatched her hand away from Rupert and went over to the window.

'All right. There was someone, when I was eighteen. He seduced me and I loved him, and he walked out on me the night my mother died.'

Rupert was unimpressed. 'But darling, one loves the most ghastly people when one's eighteen. You wouldn't be able to see what you saw in him if you met him now.'

Finally, Bella agreed to go and meet his family on her birthday, the following Thursday.

She lay in bed dreaming about Rupert the Monday morning before her birthday. I can't have been very easy these past weeks, she thought ruefully. Living on a permanent knife-edge wondering whether or not to tell him the truth about my past.

'I love you, and that's all that matters,' he'd said. Perhaps she would tell him, but could she bear to see the incredulity and contempt in his face? And if she didn't tell him, would he ever find out? No one else had. She realized that, for the first time in years, she was beginning to feel secure and happy.

She idly wondered what to wear when she met his parents. She hoped she wouldn't be too intimidated by them. She ought to buy a new dress, but too many bills were flooding in.

She picked up the paper, glanced at the gossip page to see if she or Rupert were mentioned, then turned to the personal column – villas in the South of France, ranch minks, hardly worn, costing £3,000. If I marry Rupert, she thought, they'd be within my grasp.

And then she saw the advertisement, in bold type, edged with black, and went cold with horror.

'Mabel, where are you? I've looked for you everywhere. I'll be waiting at the bar of the Hilton at seven o'clock. Steve.'

Suddenly, her heart was pounding, her hands clammy.

It must be a mistake. Lots of people communicated through

the personal column – gangs of criminals, lost friends. It was a fluke. It couldn't concern her.

But all day long she couldn't get the thought of it out of her mind.

Next day, when she picked up the paper, she tried not to turn immediately to the personal column. But there was another advertisement, burning a hole in the page.

'Mabel, where are you? Why did you leave Nalesworth? Please come to the Hilton bar at seven o'clock tonight. Steve.'

Oh God! thought Bella, giving a whimper of horror. A feeling of nausea overwhelmed her.

On Wednesday, after a sleepless night, she found another message waiting for her.

'Mabel, where are you? I waited on Monday. Perhaps you can't get to London? Cable me at the Hilton. I shall wait for you. Steve.'

She was sweating with fear. After all these years, Steve was in London, had come back to claim her. The one man in the world who could rock the boat and bring down the precarious fabrication of lies and falsehoods that was Bella Parkinson.

CHAPTER FOUR

On the morning of her birthday Bella was woken by the sun streaming through the window. For a moment she stretched luxuriously – then the sick feeling of menace overwhelmed her as she remembered Steve was trying to get in touch with her.

She jumped violently when the doorbell rang, but it was only the postman with a pile of letters and a registered parcel to be signed for. The newspaper was lying on the doormat. Willing herself not to look at it, Bella opened the parcel and gave a shriek of excitement. A pearl necklace was glittering inside. She put it on and rushed to the mirror. Even against a setting of mascara, smudged eyes and tousled hair, it looked beautiful.

'There is nothing to say except I love you,' Rupert had written in the accompanying letter. Bella gave a sigh of happiness. It was as if someone had pulled her in out of the cold and wrapped her in a mink coat.

There were cards from the rest of the cast, and more bills. There were far too many of those crowding in lately.

The telephone rang. It was Barney, her agent.

'Happy Birthday, darling. Do you feel frightfully old?'

'Yes,' said Bella.

'I'll buy you lunch next week. We can't go on not meeting like this,' said Barney.

Bella laughed. Barney always cheered her up.

'Harry Backhaus is in London casting for Anna Karenina,' he said, in his nasal cockney drawl. 'He saw you on the box last week and wants to audition you this evening.'

'But I can't,' wailed Bella. 'Not tonight. I'm meeting Rupert's family.'

'I know sweetheart. As if you'd let me forget it. I've arranged for you to see Harry beforehand – at six. He's staying at the Hyde Park. Ask for his suite at the desk. He likes birds, so be yourself. You know, sexy but refined. And don't be late.'

Bella was elated. She'd worshipped Harry Backhaus for years. She rifled through her wardrobe for something to wear, but found nothing sexy enough. She'd have to go out and buy yet another dress. Afterwards she would come back and change into the discreet but ludicrously expensive black midi dress she'd bought for meeting Rupert's parents.

The telephone rang again. This time it was Rupert wishing her a happy birthday. She thanked him ecstatically for the necklace, then told him about the audition.

'I don't know who I'm more frightened of – Harry Backhaus or your parents.'

'It won't be just them,' said Rupert. 'Gay, my sister will be there with Teddy, her fiancé.'

'What's he like?'

'He's in the Brigade. If you take away his long umbrella he falls over. His chin goes straight down into his stiff collar. Gay used to be an ally. Now all she can talk about is curtain material. I say, you'll never guess.'

'What?'

'She's pregnant.'

'My God! When did she find out?'

'Well, she only told me yesterday, so she'll have to carry a very big bouquet.'

'Was your mother livid?'

'Doesn't know. My father was very good. He walked once round the drawing-room then said, "Never mind, you always get a few shots fired before the 12th of August." '

Bella giggled.

'And as well as my pregnant sister,' Rupert went on, 'you're finally going to meet my glamorous cousin, Lazlo, and you're to promise not to fall for him; and his sister Chrissie's coming too. She's sweet. So there'll be some young people – as my mother calls them – for you to play with, darling.'

Dear Rupert, thought Bella fondly, as she put down the receiver. He loved her so much, Steve really couldn't hurt her any more. Casually, she picked up the paper. She must have been imagining things before.

But there it was – the first advertisement that caught her eyes when she turned to the personal column.

'Mabel, where are you? Why didn't you turn up at the Hilton? I shall wait again tonight. Steve.'

She felt a lurch of fear as a huge black cloud moved over the sun of her happiness.

She spent the rest of the day in a frenzy of activity – shopping and at the hairdresser. Anything not to think about Steve. She squandered a fortune on new make-up, a pair of impossibly tight blue jeans and a white frilly blouse that plunged to the waist. She also had her hair set in a wildly dishevelled style that made her look as though she'd just crawled out of bed.

She arrived twenty minutes late for the audition. Harry Backhaus turned out to be a lean, dyspeptic American who sucked peppermints all the time. He had been ruined, he said, by lunch at what was supposed to be the best restaurant in London.

'So you wanna play Anna, eh?' he said.

'I'd like to.'

'Know the book?'

'Adore it. I've read it over and over again.'

'So you've got all kinds of preconceived notions how the part should be played?'

'I could be talked out of them.'

'I picture Anna as dark. You'd have to dye your hair. You'd have to diet, too. And the boy we've got lined up for Vronsky is a good three inches shorter than you.'

Finally he said, 'We'll be in touch. Thanks for coming along.'

A beautiful tiny brunette was waiting to go in as she came out.

'Harry, darling! It's been too long!' Bella heard her say as she shut the door behind her.

Bella looked at her watch. It was twenty to seven. Enough time to go home and change before dinner. But she didn't go home. Across the Park she could see the Hilton gleaming like a liner at sea. Her flat was in the opposite direction but, as though mesmerized, she began walking towards the hotel.

You're mad, she kept telling herself. You're walking straight into a torture chamber. In five minutes you'll undo all the good of the last five years.

Just go and have a quick drink, said another voice inside her. See if it really is Steve and come away. Once you've seen him it'll break the spell.

Outside the hotel, to gain time, she bought some flowers for Rupert's mother.

Her heart was thudding like a tom-tom. Her hands were clammy as she went through the swing doors of the hotel.

The bar was very crowded. People turned to stare at her. Why couldn't she stop trembling? A tall, fair man who looked like a pig was giving her the glad eye. Surely he couldn't be Steve?

'Hullo, darling,' said a soft voice with an American accent in her ear.

She jumped like a startled horse and swung round. Her mouth was dry. The bottom seemed to fall out of her stomach as she looked into the bluest, most wicked eyes in the world.

'Oh, Baby,' he said, taking her hands. 'It's so good to see you.'

'Hullo, Steve,' she croaked.

'You made it. You really showed up. I can't believe it. Come and sit down.'

Bella felt the years melt away. She was eighteen again.

'We ought to celebrate by drinking that filthy sparkling hock which I always pretended to you was champagne.'

'I'd like some whisky,' said Bella stiffly.

'Two double Scotches,' Steve told the waiter.

He got out a packet of cigarettes and, as he lit hers, their fingers touched.

'Oh, honey,' he said. 'You've grown so beautiful. Look at me properly.'

With a great effort she raised her eyes to his. How insane she'd been to think he'd have gone off. If anything he was better looking – more seasoned. He'd lost his peachey, open, golden-boy look. There were lines now, fanning out at the corners of his eyes, and his hair was brushed forward in a thick, blond fringe to cover lines that might have developed on his forehead.

She lowered her eyes.

'I've looked for you everywhere,' he went on, as their drinks arrived. 'I wrote to Nalesworth over and over again, but they sent my letters back saying you'd gone away like a fox. I even went there to see if anyone had any news of you. Advertising in the personal columns was my last hope. What are you doing now – modelling?'

'I'm an actress.' She couldn't keep the pride out of her voice as she told him how well she'd done.

Steve whistled. 'You have gone places.'

'And I've just had an audition with Harry Backhaus for the lead in his new film.'

Lay it on thick, she thought. Damn you, Steve. I can get along without you.

'Darling, you're a star! I must come and see the play. What name do you act under? Surely not Mabel Figge?'

'No,' said Bella in a strangled voice. 'I ... I changed my name to Bella Parkinson.'

She noticed that he was wearing a very well-cut suit and heavy gold cuff-links.

'You've made good too, Steve.'

He grinned. 'Can't complain. I've got a couple of clubs in Buenos Aires. One of the reasons I'm over here – apart from finding you, of course – is to find a site for a disco in London.'

He signalled to the waiter. 'Let's have another drink.'

'Not for me,' she said. 'I can't stay.'

But she didn't move, and when the drinks came he raised his glass to her. 'To us, baby.'

'There isn't going to be any "us"!' she snapped. 'I've got someone else.'

'Did have, you mean. Who is he?'

Again the temptation to brag was too much.

'You won't know him. He's called Rupert Henriques.'

Steve raised his eyebrows. 'Not the banking family?'

Bella nodded defiantly.

'Oh, sweetheart, you *are* piling yourself up riches on earth.'

'You know him?'

'I've run across his cousin, Lazlo, in Buenos Aires.'

'Everyone seems to know him. Rupert adores him. What's he like?'

'Ruthless, rather sinister. A strange mixture. Half Jewish – his mother is some Austrian opera singer. The City don't know what to make of him. They don't approve of his long hair and all that scent he wears. But they have to admit he pulls off deals with a panache no one else can equal. He's got the kind of steel nerves that buys when the market's down. And he owns some pretty good horses.'

'Why isn't he married?'

'Doesn't believe in it. I think he got very badly burnt over some married woman several years ago. Always has the most fantastic birds, though.'

There was a pause. Then Steve went on, 'But it's Rupert you're keen on?'

'Yes I am,' said Bella quickly.

'Then why did you come here today?'

'I wanted to lay a ghost. Steve, I must go.'

How idiotic those monosyllables sounded. She had to go home, change and go out to dinner with the Henriques, but she couldn't move.

'Darling,' Steve said softly, 'I know I behaved like a heel, walking out on you when you most needed me. But I owed bread everywhere. I'd have been arrested if I'd stayed in Nalesworth any longer.'

'And what about all those other girls every night?' Impossible to keep the shrill hostility out of her voice.

'I was too young to be tied down. I've grown up since then. I wouldn't cheat on you now, if that's what you're thinking.'

But she was only conscious of his big, sexy body lounging beside her, and the fact that she wanted him as she'd never wanted anyone else.

'You're no good for me, Steve. I want to marry someone nice and stable.'

'And I'm just nice,' sighed Steve. 'One has to specialize so young these days.'

He sat back and let one of his knees rub against hers. She jumped as though she'd touched a live wire.

'My, but you're edgy,' he said.

She laughed nervously.

'When did you develop that laugh?'

'What laugh?'

He imitated it, and Bella laughed again out of nervousness.

'Yeah, like that.'

'You haven't changed a bit,' she stormed. 'You always enjoyed sending me up.'

'Your voice has changed too,' he said. 'Stage school certainly ironed out all the Yorkshire accent.'

As she leapt to her feet, he grabbed her.

'Let go of my hand,' she choked.

'Come on honey, don't be mad at me.'

'Let me go,' her voice rose.

'Keep your voice down. Everyone's looking at us. Oh, come on!' He pulled her down beside him.

'Don't you understand! I've come thousands of miles to get you back. I'm the one who knows all about you, darling. I bet you haven't told Baby Henriques about life in the slums and your jailbird father, have you?'

'Shut up!' spat Bella, turning white.

'And that's only the beginning, as you well know. Now finish up your drink like a good girl and I'll drop you off wherever you want to go. But from tomorrow the heat's on. I'm not going to let the Henriques get their hands on you. You don't want to get mixed up with them, darling; you're batting out of your league.'

As the taxi drove towards Chichester Terrace, Bella frantically combed her hair and re-did her face.

'Stop fussing,' said Steve.

'But I'm so unsuitably dressed,' wailed Bella. 'I had this lovely little black dress.'

'You're an actress. The Henriques would be terribly disappointed if you turned up looking straight. Just tell them Harry Backhaus kept you for hours, and only just let you go.'

They were driving along the Old Brompton Road now, the cherry trees dazzling white against the darkening sky.

'It's spring,' said Steve, taking her in his arms. 'Can't you feel the sap rising?'

For a moment she kissed him back, aware only of the appalling rightness of being in his arms.

'Don't go,' he whispered.

'No, Steve. For God's sake!' She pushed him violently away

and sat back trembling, unable to speak until the taxi swung into Chichester Terrace.

He wrote her telephone number down on a cigarette packet.

'Don't lose it,' she was furious to find herself saying. 'I'm ex-directory. Oh God, you've sat on Rupert's mother's flowers.'

CHAPTER FIVE

As she stood in the road, watching the taxi carry him away, she was overwhelmed by desolation. She ran past the big, white houses, set back from the road, their gardens filled with early roses and azaleas. Then she came to the whitest and biggest of all. Two stone lions with sneering faces reared up on either side of the gate. A maid answered the door, but before she could take Bella's coat Rupert rushed into the hall, his face white and drawn.

How ridiculously young and unfledged he looks beside Steve, she thought.

'Darling! What happened? It's after nine o'clock!'

Bella was not an actress for nothing. Suddenly she was the picture of distress and contrition.

'I'm so sorry! Harry Backhaus kept me waiting for ages, and then took hours over the audition, and then he made the most frightful pass at me.' Her eyes filled with tears. 'I wanted to phone, really I did, but it got so late it seemed more sensible to come straight here. I didn't even have time to change. Please forgive me.'

Any moment a thunderbolt will strike me down, she thought wryly. But Rupert, at least, was convinced.

'Poor darling,' he said, seizing her hands. 'Of course it doesn't matter. Come in and meet everyone.'

They went into a huge unwelcoming room, a cross between a museum and a jungle full of gilded furniture and elegant uncomfortable chairs. On the wall, appallingly badly lit, hung huge paintings with heavy gold frames. Potted plants were everywhere.

'Poor Bella's had a terrible time,' Rupert announced. 'The damned director's only just let her go.'

'I'm so sorry,' Bella said, giving them her most captivating smile. 'He kept me waiting for hours, and then . . .'

'We heard you saying so outside,' said a large woman coldly.
'This is my mother,' said Rupert.
Constance Henriques was tall but not thin enough. Her face, with its large turned-down mouth and bulging, glacial eyes, resembled a cod on a slab. Her voice would have carried across any parade ground.
'It's nice to meet you,' said Bella, deciding it wasn't.
'I thought you told Miss Parkinson we always dress for dinner,' Constance said to Rupert.
Bella had had too many whiskies, 'And I've undressed,' she said, looking down at her unbuttoned shirt. And, almost unconsciously slipping into a mocking upper class accent, added, 'I'm most frightfully sorry.'
There was a frozen pause, then someone laughed.
'This is my father,' said Rupert, grinning.
Charles Henriques must once have been very handsome, but had long since gone to seed. There was a network of purple veins over his face and great bags under his merry little dark eyes, which ran over Bella's *décolleté* like a pair of black beetles.
'How do you?' he said, holding her hand far longer than necessary. 'Rupert has talked about no one else for weeks. But even he didn't do you justice.'
He handed Bella a vast drink.
Rupert's sister, Gay, and her fiancé, Teddy, were a typical deb and a typical guards officer. They hardly broke off their conversation when Bella was introduced to them.
Bella couldn't resist staring at Gay's stomach. She didn't look at all pregnant – nor did Teddy look capable of fathering a mouse.
'I told you they were totally self-obsessed, didn't I?' Rupert said, squeezing her hand. 'And finally I want you to meet my cousin Chrissie, Lazlo's sister. She's my good angel.'
She'd be divine too, if she were happier, thought Bella. But Chrissie looked thoroughly out of condition. Her dark eyes were puffy, a spot glowed on her cheek, and she must have put on a lot of weight recently because the dress she was wearing was far too tight over her heavy bust and hips.
'How do you do?' Chrissie said. She had a soft, husky voice with a slight foreign inflection. 'How foul having an audition. They must be beastly things.'

'I always get into a state,' said Bella, 'but some people sail through them.'

Chrissie started to talk about a friend who wanted to go on the stage but, although her mouth smiled, her eyes looked at Bella with hatred.

Bella gulped her drink and looked round the room. That was certainly a Matisse over the fireplace and a Renoir by the door. Between the curtains there was a lighter square on the rose-coloured wallpaper.

'The Gainsborough usually hangs there,' said Constance, following Bella's gaze, 'But we've lent it to the Royal Academy. What can Lazlo be talking about all this time?' she added irritably to Charles. 'The telephone bills that boy runs up.'

'He's talking to some Arabs,' said Rupert. 'He's been trying to get through all day.'

'How exciting to have a wedding so soon,' Bella said brightly.

They all looked at her. I'd better shut up, she thought. My girlish approach is going down like a lead balloon.

'It's your birthday, isn't it? How old are you?' said Constance Henriques, her mouth full of potato crisps.

'Twenty-four,' replied Bella.

'Twenty-four? But Rupert's only twenty-one. I'd no idea you were so much older than him.'

'And you've just turned fifty-four, my dear,' said Charles Henriques mildly. 'So I think the less said about age the better.'

Bella giggled, which was obviously the wrong thing to do, for Constance Henriques had turned the colour of a turkey cock.

Fortunately there was the click of a telephone.

'That'll be Lazlo finished,' said Constance. 'We can eat at least. It's too much to expect the young to be punctual these days, but I do hate keeping the servants waiting.'

Bella flushed. Rupert's mother was a cow. Thank God Lazlo was going to join them now. Of all the Henriques family he was the one she felt she was going to get on with. She imagined a gay, laughing, handsome, more dissipated version of Rupert, with the same slenderness and delicate features. But as usual in such cases, she couldn't have been more wrong in her assessment.

For the man who came through the door was tall and as powerfully built as Steve. With his sallow complexion, hooked nose, thick black curling hair and drooping eyelids, it was difficult to tell if he looked more South American or more Jewish in his appearance. But there was certainly nothing of the Jewish fleshiness about his face, nor the melting softness of the Latin about his eyes, which were as hard and black as tarmac. He looked dangerous and incredibly tough.

Rupert bounded forward, 'Lazlo! Bella's arrived. Come and meet her.'

Wincing slightly at the pride in Rupert's voice, Bella gave Lazlo her most seductive smile. 'I've heard so much about you,' she said. 'I feel I know you very well already.'

For a second there was a flicker of surprise in his eyes. He certainly took his time to look her over. Then, with a smile that wasn't entirely friendly, he said, 'I can assure you you don't. How do you do?'

Then he turned to Constance.

'Sorry I took so long. This deal's reached a really delicate stage. If we pull it off though, Charles'll make enough bread to pay for Gay's wedding.'

Constance didn't look in the least mollified. But at that moment a maid announced dinner was ready.

Until then Bella had drunk enough whisky to sail through any situation, but as they went into the dining-room she was overwhelmed with a fear so violent that she had to clutch on to the table to stop herself fainting.

What was that terrible sickly smell? Then she realized it was the lilies – a huge clump was massed on a Grecian pillar at the far end of the room and another great bowl filled the centre of the table.

Bella stared at them horrified, remembering the wreaths of lilies that had filled the house before her mother's funeral, just after Steve had walked out on her. And how closely, at the time, the white waxy petals had resembled the translucence of her mother's skin as she lay dead upstairs. She felt the sweat rising on her forehead. She was trembling all over.

Looking up, she saw Lazlo watching her. Immediately on the defensive she glared back, then cursed herself as he looked away. It would have been so much more politic to smile.

They sat down at a table that could easily have accommodated a couple of dozen people. Bella was between Charles and Teddy. Rupert was hidden from her by the centrepiece of lilies. A maid began handing round a great bucket of caviar.

Constance and Gay discussed the wedding.

'It's amazing how people cough up,' said Gay. 'The most unlikely relations have sent vast cheques.'

'When I was married,' said Constance, taking a far bigger helping than anyone else, 'all the West Wing was cordoned off to accommodate the presents. I'd forgotten how much there is to do. I'm quite exhausted. I've been tied up with the bishop all afternoon.'

'How very uncomfortable for you both,' said Lazlo gravely.

Constance ignored this. 'The bishop was most impressed by our work for the blind,' she went on. 'Particularly with the number of new guide dogs we've provided.'

Lazlo held up his wine so that it gleamed like a pool of gold. 'You should start a society of Guide People for Blind Dogs,' he said.

'Do you know Baby Ifield?' Charles shouted to Bella down six feet of polished mahogany.

She shook her head.

'Should have seen her in her heyday. My word she was a smasher. Used to go back stage and see her. Often took her to the Four Hundred.'

Constance's lips tightened.

'I simply can't bear to discuss the mess this government is making,' she said, and proceeded to do so for half an hour.

Listening to her, Bella found herself becoming more and more critical, and as her critical spirit waxed, her tact and caution waned.

Constance switched to the subject of Northern Ireland. 'If only they'd bring back hanging.'

'Why should they?' said Bella, her trained actress's voice carrying down the table.

Constance looked at her as though one of the potatoes had spoken.

'It'd soon stop them dropping bombs so casually,' said Constance.

'No way,' said Bella. 'There's nothing the Irish like better than feeling martyred. Hanging would only make them step up the campaign.'

Constance was revving up for a really crushing reply, when Lazlo said,

'How's Jonathan?'

'A case in point,' said Constance sourly. 'Young people today are allowed far too much freedom. His housemaster wrote to me only this morning saying Jonathan painted "Death to Apartheid" in red all over the chapel wall.'

Lazlo and Charles grinned. Rupert started to laugh.

'But that's great,' said Bella, whose glass had been filled for the fourth time. 'He's doing something positive.'

Constance stared at Bella, her cold eyes baleful. 'Have you ever been to South Africa?'

'No,' admitted Bella.

'I thought not. People who haven't first-hand knowledge of a country always make sweeping generalizations.'

'But one has only to read the papers ...' Bella was thoroughly roused by now.

'I bought that chestnut filly I told you about, Charles.' Once more Lazlo had interrupted her in mid-sentence.

Suddenly, the table came to life. Horses were obviously a complete obsession where the Henriques were concerned.

The candles threw sharp daggers of light on to the table. Chrissie was talking to Rupert. Bella watched the rapt expression on the girl's face.

So that's the way the wind blows, she thought. No wonder she hates me.

Constance was rabbiting on about the game reserves. Lazlo was picking his teeth.

I was a fool to come, thought Bella miserably. Steve was right about these people.

She felt both exhausted and depressed when they left the men to their port and cigars. Chrissie sat down at the grand piano and played Beethoven extremely well.

She looks beautiful now, thought Bella, looking at her softened face, the lamplight on the black hair.

Constance and Gay talked more about the wedding, Constance sewing a piece of tapestry of a Victorian lady with a hare lip.

Rupert joined them first and came straight over to Bella, his face drawn.

'All right, darling?'

'Fine,' snapped Bella. 'Give me a cigarette.' She was irritated that he hadn't stuck up for her at dinner.

'Sorry we took so long,' he said. 'My father and Lazlo were having rather a heated discussion about devaluation.'

But Lazlo didn't look heated as he came through the door a moment later, smoking a large cigar and laughing at some joke of Charles's, his saturnine face lit up by the glitter of dark eyes and the flash of very white teeth.

He ought to laugh more, thought Bella, as he went over to the piano.

'All right, love?' Lazlo picked up a loose hair from Chrissie's shoulder.

'Of course,' she said brightly.

'Good.' He smiled down at her, then crossed the room and sat down beside Bella.

He's a womanizer, thought Bella. Maybe I'll try and vamp him. She leaned forward to show him more of her cleavage.

'I met a friend of yours the other day,' he said.

'Oh, who?' said Bella, giving him a long, hot, lingering glance, which was immediately wiped off her face when he said, 'Angora Fairfax. She said you were at drama school together.'

Bella had always loathed Angora Fairfax. She had been the spoilt darling of immensely rich parents, always at parties and complaining how exhausted she was next morning. All her fellow students, except Bella, had been pixillated by her. Angora, in her turn, had been jealous of Bella's talent.

'I knew her slightly,' said Bella. 'What's she up to now?'

'A television series, I think. She talked a lot about you.'

'I'm sure,' said Bella coldly.

'She's extremely attractive,' said Lazlo, examining his whisky. 'Can she act?'

Bella nodded. She wasn't going to fall into the trap of being bitchy.

'I hear you had an audition tonight,' Lazlo went on.

Bella's early warning system wasn't working very well.

'Yes, I did.'

'And the director made a pass at you. How distressing for you.'

Sarcastic cat, thought Bella.

'Who was he?'

'Harry Backhaus.'

'Harry?' His eyebrows shot up. 'Unlike him. He's only just got married again. We're lunching tomorrow. I'll give him a bollocking.'

Bella felt herself going hot, then cold, with horror.

'Oh, no! please don't,' she said, far too quickly. 'I expect he got carried away.'

Lazlo's smile was bland. 'Still, there's no excuse for that sort of thing.'

At half past eleven Bella got up to go.

'I'll drive you home,' said Rupert.

'I'll take her,' said Lazlo. 'I go straight past her door.'

'But it's not that way,' said Rupert mutinously.

'I'd like you to wait for another call from Sordid Arabia,' said Lazlo. 'You know the background.'

Wow! thought Bella, he's really pulling rank. And she willed Rupert to stand up to him. But Rupert opened his mouth, shut it again, and sulkily agreed.

As she left, Charles kissed her on both cheeks. 'We'll see you at the wedding next month, if not before,' he said.

Everyone stiffened. 'Have you sent Bella an invitation yet, Constance?' he added.

'We've run out,' said Constance coldly.

'Nonsense. There are at least a dozen left in your desk. We need a bit of glamour on our side of the church.'

When they were nearing Bella's flat, Lazlo said, 'I want to talk to you. Shall we go to your flat or mine?'

'I'm very tired,' snapped Bella. 'Can't we talk here?'

'No,' he said. 'It's important.'

'All right. We'd better use mine.'

Her flat was in chaos, clothes all over the drawing-room, unwashed breakfast things lying around. Bella kicked a bra under the sofa and went into the bedroom to take off her coat. In the mirror her eyes glittered with drink. Really, that blouse was too indecent for words. Perhaps Lazlo was going to make a pass at her. When she came back she found him sprawled in an armchair playing with the solitaire board.

He's got the face of a riverboat gambler, she thought, tough, cool, measuring up all the options.

'Did Rupert give you this?' he said.

Bella nodded.

'He's a nice boy,' said Lazlo.

'*I* think so,' said Bella. 'Do you want a drink?'

Lazlo shook his head. 'Rupert hasn't had an easy life,' he went on. 'Lots of spoiling but not much love. Constance has always been too tied up with her charities; Charles much too preoccupied with Old Masters and young mistresses. Rupert's pretty unstable as a result. He needs someone who can't only handle him, but who also loves him very much.'

'My,' said Bella with a nervous laugh, 'I didn't know you were that romantic.'

Lazlo didn't smile back. 'I'm not. I just hate waste.'

Bella took a deep breath. 'You don't want me to marry him, do you?'

'No, I don't.'

'Because I don't come out of the top drawer?'

'I don't care if you come out of the coal-hole! I just want Rupert to land up with someone who loves him.'

'Like your sister Chrissie, I suppose? Then you'd keep all your millions in the family.'

'Leave Chrissie out of it.'

'Why should I? What makes you think she loves Rupert more than I do?'

'She wouldn't have arrived an hour late to meet her future mother-in-law.'

'I told you I couldn't get away. I was stuck at the audition.'

'And not bothered to dress.'

'I didn't have time to change.'

'Or arrived three parts cut.'

'I was not. Americans just pour very strong drinks.'

'Or been rude to Aunt Constance on every possible occasion.'

'She was insufferable,' said Bella in a choked voice.

'I agree,' he said evenly. 'She's an uphill battle-axe. But if you loved Rupert you'd have put up with it.'

'What's it got to do with you, anyway?' Bella said furiously.

He had only a few marbles left now in the centre of the solitaire board. She watched his long fingers, mesmerized.

'All I'm saying,' he said softly, 'is that if you loved Rupert, you'd have arrived on time, sober, properly dressed, instead of swilling whisky in the Hilton Bar with one of your lovers.'

Bella turned green. 'W . . . what are you talking about?' she whispered. 'I was having an audition.'

'Maybe you were earlier in the evening, baby. But when I saw you, you were so engrossed with your handsome desperado, you didn't even notice I was sitting only a few tables away.'

Confusion and horror swept over her. Lazlo had seen her with Steve. How much had he heard of their conversation?

'He's an actor,' she lied quickly. 'We . . . er . . . we were discussing a play we're doing together next week.'

'Rehearsing all the love scenes,' said Lazlo dryly. 'If you gazed at Rupert with a tenth of that slavish adoration, I'd be only too happy for you to marry him.'

He was left with one dark green marble now. He looked at it for a moment, then, putting the board down, took out his cheque book.

'Now,' he said, in a businesslike tone. 'How much do you want? If I give you – oh, five grand, will you leave Rupert alone?'

Bella laughed in spite of herself. 'I never realized people really said things like that! No, I won't.'

'Because you adore Rupert and can't live without him?' he said acidly.

'I never said anything about love,' she said. 'It's you who keeps banging on about it. But since you want things spelled out – I don't intend to break it off!'

'Ten grand,' said Lazlo.

There was a pause. Bella looked out of the window.

Wow, the things I could do with ten thousand pounds, she thought. I wonder if it would be tax free? Then aloud she said,

'I don't want your rotten money. You'll have to think of something else.'

Lazlo put away his cheque book and got to his feet. The sheer size of him made her step back. 'Well, if you won't be sensible about it, I shall have to try other methods.'

'You can't stop me marrying Rupert.'

'I can't?' he said softly. 'You obviously can't be familiar with our family motto: "Scratch a Henriques and you draw your own blood." '

The long scar showed white on his swarthy skin. A shiver ran down Bella's spine.

He's like the devil, she thought.

'My family's got a lot of influence,' he went on. 'We can make things very difficult for you if you don't play ball.'

'You're threatening me?' she said.

'Yes, and I'd warn you, I fight very dirty. Are you sure you don't want that cheque?'

Bella lost her temper. 'Get out! Get out!' she screamed. And, picking up a blue glass bowl, she hurled it at him. But he ducked and it smashed on the wall behind him. He laughed and left.

Bella couldn't stop shaking after he'd gone.

Oh no, she wailed. Why did I blow my top? Loathsome, horrible bully. He's only bluffing. He wouldn't do anything really.

And yet ... and yet ... with all that money and power behind him ...

She shivered with fear. Perhaps she ought to take the money and clear out with Steve. But Steve was unreliable, not to be trusted. And then, of course, there was poor Rupert to be considered.

Suddenly the doorbell rang, making her jump out of her skin. Lazlo again? Steve? Her heart was cracking her ribs. Whoever it was was leaning on the bell.

'Who is it?' she sobbed in terror.

'It's me, Rupert.'

She opened the door and, as he followed her inside, she burst into a storm of weeping.

'Darling! Hush, sweetheart! It went all right.' He pulled her down beside him on the sofa, stroking her hair. 'They're always bloody at first. You should have seen them with Teddy. Wasn't Lazlo nice to you?'

She shook her head. She hadn't meant to tell Rupert, but she couldn't control herself any more.

'He hates me,' she sobbed. 'More than any of them. He said he doesn't want me to marry you.'

'He doesn't? Probably fancies you, that's why he's so rude. Anyway, my father's crazy about you.'

How good it was to be held in his arms and comforted.

'I'm so rotten to you,' she muttered. 'Arriving late and cheeking your mother. I don't know why you put up with me.'

And you don't know the half of it, she thought miserably.

'There's nothing to put up with,' Rupert said. 'I love you ten times more than I did this morning. I'd kill anyone who hurt you.'

She moved away and looked at him. Harlequin's face, sad, pale, with great blue rings under his eyes.

'Bella, darling, please let's get married.'

And whether it was to spite Lazlo, or to escape from Steve, or because she was drunk, or because Rupert wanted her so much she never knew, but the next moment she was saying yes.

CHAPTER SIX

BELLA woke next morning with a series of flashbulbs exploding in her head. Scenes from last night's débâcle re-staged themselves with relentless accuracy – the disastrous audition with Harry Backhaus, the meeting with Steve, the catastrophic dinner party at the Henriques'. She was just wincing her way through that appalling moment when she'd hurled a glass bowl at Lazlo, when she sat bolt upright and gave a groan.

Jesus! She'd let herself get engaged to Rupert. But she didn't love Rupert. She loved Steve – and that snake Lazlo Henriques knew it too, and would pull out every stop to make her break it off with Rupert.

Oh God, she wailed, pulling the bedclothes over her head, what a terrible mess!

The events of the next weeks left her breathless. Rupert insisted on looking at dozens of houses, taking her on a triumphal round of his relations and showering her with presents – including a huge plastic pink, heart-shaped engagement ring because he knew it would irritate his mother.

Bella had expected Lazlo to come round breathing fire, but he did nothing, obviously biding his time. What really crucified her was that even though Steve must have read about her engagement – every paper splashed pictures of 'The Millionaire and the Showgirl' – he made no attempt to get in touch with her.

The sex side with Rupert hadn't been going well either. Now she was engaged, she could hardly refuse to sleep with him. Rupert, fobbed off for so long, wanted to spend every free moment in bed, then afterwards was desperate for reassurance.

'Was it all right, darling? Are you sure it was all right for you?'

'Yes, yes,' she would say, pulling him down on to her breast until he fell asleep, and she would gaze unseeingly at the ceiling, her body twitching with unsatisfied desire and longing for Steve.

A week later, after a performance at the theatre, she slumped down in front of her dressing-room mirror, cheers echoing in her ears. She had acted superbly. Now she was all in.

Rupert had gone to a dinner in the city and wasn't meeting her until later. It gave her a breathing space.

Convincing him how blissfully happy she was to be marrying him put more of a strain on her than anything else.

Dully, she reached for a pot of cleansing cream to take off her make-up. There was a knock on the door.

'Come in,' she said, listlessly.

Then her heart gave a sickening lurch. Steve stood in the doorway – lazy, smiling, impossibly blond and handsome.

'How did you get in here?' she gasped.

'The doorman's a mate of mine.' He shut the door and leaned against it. 'Well?' he added softly.

'Well, what?'

'I thought I told you not to get tangled up with Rupert Henriques.'

'It's nothing to do with you!' There was a sob in her voice. 'A lot you care. You haven't even rung me.'

'I thought I'd leave you on slow burn for a week or two,' he said.

He walked towards her and put a hand on her bare shoulder. Funny how Rupert could maul her for hours and nothing happened, but just a touch from Steve sent a thousand volts through her. The warm hand crept slowly up her shoulder round to the back of her neck.

Then he laughed. 'You were fantastic as Desdemona, honey. I'd no idea you were that good.'

Happiness flooded through her. 'Oh! Did you really think so?'

'Yes. Absolutely bowled me over,' he said, bending his head and kissing her.

Bella was kissing him back. His hand was edging down the front of her dress and everything was getting quite out of control when, suddenly, to her horror, she heard the door burst open and a voice saying, 'This must be Bella's room.'

Colour flooding her face, she leapt away from Steve – but it was too late. Standing in the doorway was Lazlo Henriques and Bella's old enemy from drama school, Angora Fairfax.

'Bella. You are frightful,' said Angora with a giggle. 'You've only just got engaged to Rupert and here you are being unfaithful already with this stunning man.' She raised her huge blue eyes to Steve. 'I think you should call him out,' she added to Lazlo.

'Rupert can fight his own battles,' said Lazlo, looking amused. 'Hello, Bella. How are you?'

Bella was speechless. It was Steve who came to the rescue.

'I'd better introduce myself. My name's Steve Benedict,' he said, grinning.

'And I'm Angora Fairfax. And this foxy individual here is Lazlo Henriques,' said Angora.

She was as pretty as a kitten, incredibly slim with tiny wrists and ankles, cloudy dark hair, purply-blue eyes and pouting red lips which didn't quite meet over her slightly protruding teeth. Angora, said one of her stage school colleagues, was the sort of girl who could get away with asking a man if he could 'possibly carry this frightfully heavy match box'.

'Bella, darling,' she said. 'Do stop looking so pink in the face. It was a lovely performance. You were so good – though they shouldn't have given you that terrible set in the last act. I mean you were hopping all over the place like the Grand National. Lazlo was awful. He went to sleep in the second and third acts, but he's had a rough day. Gold bullion's gone down a halfpenny or something. Have you anything for us to drink?'

'Yes, of course,' said Bella, grinding her teeth. She'd forgotten Angora's ability to make her feel a complete idiot. 'There's a bottle of whisky in the cupboard. Perhaps you'd do the honours, Steve.'

When Steve had poured out four very large drinks, Lazlo raised his glass to Bella. 'To you and Rupert,' he said, with a nasty glint in his eye.

'Yes, to the lovebirds,' said Angora. 'You must be in a daze of happiness, Bella. Such a relief to be settled and know one won't end up a terrible old maid keeping cats in a garret.' She looked at Lazlo under long, sooty black lashes.

'Don't fish, Angora,' he said.

She giggled. 'I'm sorry, but I'm a bit over-excited. Harry Backhaus has signed me up for the lead in his new film.'

'That's great,' said Steve, flashing her his devastating smile. 'How did you pull that off?'

'Strings really, darling. Lazlo took me and Harry out to a long, drunken lunch today. I gather you went after the part too, Bella darling? But as they start shooting in a fortnight, I knew you wouldn't want to be parted from Rupert so soon.'

'Of course I wouldn't!' said Bella. And she smiled at Lazlo, her heart black with hatred.

'What about you then?' Angora said to Steve. 'Where did Bella dig up something as lovely as you from?'

'Buenos Aires,' said Steve. He turned to Lazlo. 'Actually, we've met. I own the Amontillado Club. You've been in once or twice.'

'One of my favourite haunts,' said Lazlo. 'It's so dark I can never remember who I've come in with.'

'Is it nice out there?' asked Angora.

'It's nice anywhere,' said Steve and, laughing, he refilled Lazlo's glass.

Bella suddenly felt twitchy. If Lazlo learned from Steve the real truth about her past, heaven knows what use he'd make of it.

Angora was rabbiting on and on about acting. Steve and Lazlo had moved on to business.

'Money, money, money!' said Angora finally. 'I can see you two are going to be very bad for each other.'

Bella felt a stab of jealousy. In a quarter of an hour they'd accepted Steve as they'd never accept her.

He was talking to Angora now, turning on his *homme fatal* act, dropping his voice several semi-tones, flashing his teeth all over the place.

Finally, Angora stretched. 'Lazlo, darling. If I don't eat I shall fall over.'

'Let's go then,' said Lazlo, stubbing out his cigar. 'Why don't you come, too?' he added to Steve.

'Won't I be *de trop*?' said Steve.

'Not at all,' said Angora. 'Lazlo will melt into a telephone box and magic up some amazing looking girl for you, then we'll go on the town. Thanks for drinks, Bella. See you at Gay's wedding. Lazlo had some crazy scheme for us all to go down to the country the next day, then we can go to Goodwood. If you like horses,' she added to Steve, 'you'd better come too.'

And they drifted out, hardly bothering to say goodbye, leaving Bella jibbering with misery and impotent rage. Lazlo's nasty grin stayed with her, like the Cheshire Cat, long after he'd gone.

She had even more cause to be angry with him in the next few days. Two television plays and a commercial she'd considered certainties suddenly fell through. Her bank manager wrote a vitriolic letter complaining about her overdraft.

She was also due to play Nina in the Britannia's production of *The Seagull*, which was going into rehearsal next week. Suddenly, Roger Field, the director, sent for her and told her he wanted her to play Masha, the frumpy, frustrated schoolmistress instead.

Bella lost her temper. 'Lazlo Henriques is behind this!' she stormed.

'Who's he?' said Roger unconvincingly. 'I make the decisions round here. I feel you'd be better as Masha.'

CHAPTER SEVEN

As usual, Bella left buying something to wear to Gay's wedding to the last minute. She knew she shouldn't buy anything at all. There were stacks of hardly worn dresses in her wardrobe and, with the present intransigence of her bank manager, he was bound to bounce the cheque anyway.

But for the last week she'd been spending money as though it was going out of fashion, almost as though she was determining her own destiny, forcing herself into such financial straits that the only way out would be to marry Rupert.

Anyway, she had to have a new dress. She knew that Steve had been asked to the wedding, and that he'd been seeing a lot of Angora, and that she must knock him for six by looking even more glamorous.

The shopping expedition was a disaster; half the shops seemed to have sales on. Everything she tried on looked perfectly frightful and she'd no idea how the weather was going to turn out. It was one of those grey, dull days that might easily get hot later.

'Puce is going to be very big in the autumn,' said a sales girl, forcing her into a wool dress and holding great folds of material in at the back to give it the appearance of fitting.

Bella winced at her washed out reflection. 'I look like something the cat brought in or up,' she said. 'I need a new face, not a new dress.'

By two o'clock, when she was getting desperate, she found a dress in willow green, sleeveless, low cut and clinging, with a wrap-over skirt. It was the only remotely sexy thing she had tried on.

'Do you think it's all right for a wedding?' she said desperately.

'Oh yes,' said the sales girl, raking a midge bite with long red nails. 'People wear anything for anything these days.'

By the time she'd found a floppy, coral pink picture hat and shoes to match she was really running out of time. But when she tried them all on later in daylight in her flat, she realized the coral looked terrible with her tawny hair.

She had an hour and a half before she had to be at the church. Her hairdresser was closed that afternoon. The only answer was to wash her hair and put a red rinse on it, but in her haste she forgot to read the instructions about not using it on dyed hair. The result was not a gentle Titian, but a bright orange going on Heinz tomato, and impossibly fluffy with it.

She soon realized, too, that half a ton of eye-liners, blushers, shaders and all her skill at making-up wasn't going to do her any good. It simply wasn't an on-day.

Her skin looked dead, her eyes small and tired, and no amount of pancake could conceal the bags under them.

It was also getting colder. A sharp east wind was flattening the leaves of the plane trees in the square outside. All her coats were too short to wear over her new dress. In the end she slung Basil, her red fox fur, round her neck.

'I need a few allies to face that mob,' she thought.

A large crowd had gathered outside the church to watch people arrive. Bella, hopelessly late, rolled up at the same time as the bridal car and fell up the steps in her haste to get in first.

'Drunk already,' said a wag in the crowd.

Lazlo helped her to her feet. With a flash of irritation she realized that he looked very good and that the austere black and white formality of morning dress suited his sallow skin and irregular features extremely well.

He looked at her hair and said, 'Oh dear, oh dear,' and then at her bare arms, and added in amusement, 'You're going to be bloody cold in church.'

She wanted to slip unnoticed into a pew at the back, but, grabbing her arm like a vice, Lazlo led her right up to the second row from the front,

'You're a member of the family now,' he said.

Rupert, looking glamorous, and almost as pale as the white carnation in his button hole, tried to sit next to her, but Lazlo stopped him.

'Uh-uh,' he said. 'You've got to sit in the front and look after

Constance,' and sat down very firmly on the edge of the row, next to Bella. Bella moved quickly away from him, slap into a very lecherous-looking old man with long grey sideboards, on her other side.

'You haven't met Uncle Willy yet, have you Bella?' said Lazlo.

Beyond Rupert sat a scruffy, but nice-looking boy with a pudding basin hair cut. That must be Rupert's brother, Jonathan, let off from school.

Across the aisle sat Teddy and his best man. Teddy's pink and white cheeks were stained with colour as he alternately tugged at his collar and smoothed his newly cut hair.

'I comforted my mother,' said Rupert, 'that she wasn't losing a daughter, just gaining a cretin.'

Bella giggled. People were turning round and talking to each other and saying, 'Hello, haven't seen you for *years*.'

The organ was playing the same Bach cantata for the third time. Bella, sneaking a surreptitious look round, realized that as usual she was quite wrongly dressed. Everyone was in silk dresses or beautifully cut suits. And the competition was absolutely stupendous. Lazlo was right; it was icy in church. Every goose pimple was standing out on her bare arms. Uncle Willy next door was gazing openly at her breasts. Irritably, to obscure his view, Bella shoved the fox's mask down the front of her dress.

'Gone to earth,' said Lazlo.

Bella gazed stonily ahead at the huge Constance Spry flower arrangement. Suddenly she realized that her wrap-over dress, which looked so respectable when she was standing up, had fallen open, revealing a large expanse of thigh and the pants with 'Abandon Hope All Ye Who Enter Here' printed on them, which Rosie had given her for her birthday. Hastily she covered herself up, but not before both Lazlo and Uncle Willy had had a good look.

I'll kill him, fumed Bella, I'll kill him, and afterwards I'll kick his teeth in.

Another old relation, sleeping peacefully behind them, suddenly woke up and said, 'Come on, buck up. Let's get cracking,' in a loud voice. There was a rustle of interest as Constance swept up the aisle looking like a double-decker bus in a dust sheet, waving graciously to friends and relations.

'She claims she's just discovered the tent dress,' Rupert whispered to Bella. 'But she needs a couple of marquees to cover her.'

Finally, when Bella was about to turn into a pillar of ice, the organ launched into 'Here Comes the Bride' and everyone rose to their feet.

Here was Charles, a fatuous smile on his face, wafting brandy fumes as he went. On his arm hung Gay, looking pale but well in control, and carrying a huge bouquet to conceal any evidence of pregnancy. Her progress was slow, for every few seconds she nearly had her head jerked off as one of the little bridesmaids trod on her veil.

Chrissie brought up the rear, wearing pink, a coronet of pink roses on her gleaming dark hair. She'd obviously had a professional make-up. She looked lovely, but suicidal. She halted just beside Lazlo. Rupert turned round and pulled a face at her, trying to make her laugh.

'Dearly beloved,' intoned the bishop.

Bella had to share a prayer book with Lazlo. Rigid with loathing, she looked down at his long fingers and beautifully manicured nails and tried not to breathe in the subtle musk and lavender overtones of the after-shave he was wearing.

'First,' said the bishop, 'it was ordained for the procreation of children.'

'You can say that again,' muttered Rupert with a grin.

'Second as a remedy against sin, for such people as have not the gift of continence.'

'I do hope you're taking all this in,' said Lazlo out of the corner of his mouth.

Bella was not listening; she was having a daydream of standing in Gay's place, with long white satin arms and hair drawn back to show a delicately blushing face, with an impossibly slender waist from a pre-wedding crash diet, with Steve beside her, devastatingly handsome, smiling proudly down at her, and putting a gold ring on her finger.

'To have and to hold, for richer for poorer, in sickness and in health, to love and to cherish till death us do part,' repeated Teddy in his strangulated hernia voice, after the bishop.

But would Steve ever stay with her? Was he capable of loving and cherishing anyone for very long? Would she herself ever be able to love and cherish Rupert the way Chrissie would?

Looking past Lazlo, she saw Chrissie staring fixedly in front of her, the tears pouring down her face. Oh, what a stupid muddle it all is, thought Bella.

'I feel sick,' said one of the little bridesmaids.

'Immortal, Invisible God only wise,' sang the congregation. Lazlo, next to her, sang the bass part loudly. He's just the sort of person who would embarrass his children singing parts too loudly in church, she thought savagely.

They all sat down for the sermon. The bishop was getting warmed up about fidelity and the need for steadfastness in the modern world when so many marriages crumbled.

Uncle Willy was rubbing his thigh against Bella's. She couldn't move away or she would have been jammed against Lazlo.

She gazed furiously in front of her. Really, she was getting to know that flower arrangement extremely well. Suddenly, with the spontaneity that was so much part of his charm, Rupert turned round, took her hand and squeezed it. She was conscious of both Lazlo and Chrissie watching them. A deep blush spread over her face and down her shoulders.

Constance was crying unashamedly as they all went off into the vestry.

'It's not because she's losing Gay,' said Lazlo dryly, 'but the thought of all the money this is costing her.'

A reedy tenor began to sing, 'Sheep May Safely Graze.'

The wait was interminable.

'You'd think they were consummating the marriage, wouldn't you?' said Rupert. 'I wish we could smoke.'

Back came the procession. Teddy, crimson with embarrassment; Gay, looking relieved, grinning slightly as she caught the eyes of various relations.

'Hear you're an actress,' said Uncle Willy to Bella. 'Ever bin in Crossroads?' (He pronounced it Crawse.) 'Never miss it m'self, bloody good programme.'

For several minutes they were penned up at the top of the church while the photographers took pictures. As soon as he came out of his pew, Rupert squeezed Bella's arm.

'Christ, what a performance. Hullo, Aunt Vera. I'm not

going through a bloody circus like this when we get married, darling. Hullo Uncle Bertie. It's going to be in and out of Chelsea Registry office and straight off to London Airport to somewhere warm immediately afterwards.'

Bella put her hand lovingly over Rupert's. 'I agree,' she said, looking straight at Lazlo. 'And as soon as possible too. I've suddenly gone off long engagements.'

The reception was a nightmare. It was held in three huge marquees in the Henriques' garden and Bella had never felt more lonely or out of things in her life.

There was a strange assortment of people there. Teddy's grand, dowdy relations in their silk shirtwaisters and pull-on felts were almost indistinguishable from Constance's fellow committee workers, who included several Chief Guiders in uniform, who brayed to one another and drank orange juice. In one corner, two bus-loads of tenants from Teddy's father's estate sat with their legs apart, looking embarrassed. But by far the largest group of people there, Bella suspected, were Charles's and Lazlo's friends, members of the international set at their richest and most international. Even though some of them had turned up in jeans, they had that kind of bland self-assurance, the gilt-edged security that enabled them to be accepted anywhere. Everywhere you looked ravishingly pretty women had emerged from their winter furs like butterflies and stood jamming cigarettes into their scarlet lips, knocking back champagne, refusing asparagus rolls and smoked salmon for the sake of their figures, and chattering wittily to the suave handsome, expensive-looking men who surrounded them. Bella had never seen so many people who seemed to know each other, or, even if they didn't, would discover a host of friends they had in common.

Rupert did his best to look after her, but he was constantly being grabbed by Constance or Charles, or particularly by Lazlo, to go and look after someone else, or see to something.

She tried to scintillate and be amusing, but because she was nervous and unsure of herself, her voice came out far more artificial and affected than it would normally. Putting up a front to cover up her desperate insecurity, she knew she was appearing phoney and as hard as nails. Rupert kept introducing her into a group of people, but it was like feeding a screw into the hoover. Five minutes later they'd spew her out again.

God, they were noisy too. Half the conversations were being carried on in foreign languages, full of laughter and exclamation marks, like the talking bits in Fidelio.

She couldn't even get drunk because she had a performance that evening. In her misery, she ate five éclairs, then felt sick.

Suddenly, as though someone had stamped a branding iron on her back, she was aware of Chrissie standing behind her, her eyes glittering with misery and loathing.

'Pink really suits you,' Bella said nervously. 'And you've lost so much weight! You really look ravishing.'

'But not quite ravishing enough,' snapped Chrissie, and, turning on her heel, she disappeared into the crowd. Even talking to Uncle Willy would have been preferable to standing by herself, but he was hemmed in by some aunts in a corner.

Where on earth were Steve and Angora, Bella wondered. It was almost impossible to find them in this crowd.

She couldn't stay leaning against a pillar for ever – like a small boat launching itself on a rough sea, she began fighting her way across the marquee again – and, suddenly, there like something on the big screen, was Angora, wearing a navy blue straw hat which framed her cloudy dark hair and a parma violet suit, which emphasized her huge, purply-blue eyes.

She was surrounded by men, but lounging by her side was Steve in a grey morning suit, cracking jokes, deflecting any competition, very much master of the situation. Admire her, but keep your distance, he seemed to be saying. They made a sensational pair.

Angora was laughing at something he said, throwing back her head to show her lovely white throat when, in mid-laugh, suddenly she saw Bella.

'Belladonna! Come here – at once.'

As there was nowhere else to go, Bella went up to them.

'Darling, you've gone orange. How brave of you. Is it for a new part, or are you doing a soup commercial?'

The men around Angora looked at Bella without interest.

'You've all met Rupert's fiancée, haven't you?' said Angora. 'You know Steve of course, Bella, and this is Timmie, and this is Patrick, and this is . . . oh God, I can't remember your name.'

Bella was looking at Steve. Her heart was pounding.

'Yes, I know Steve,' she said. 'Or I thought I did. How are you?'

'Fantastic,' said Steve, giving her that curiously opaque, shutters-down look she knew of old. 'Where's Rupert? Getting some aunt out of mothballs?'

'I'm glad you've brought Foxy,' said Angora, patting Bella's fox fur. 'He looks as though he needs an outing. Why don't you give him some Bob Martins?'

Everyone laughed. Bella blushed. Why can't I think of some witty crack to make back, she thought miserably.

Rescue, however, was at hand, in the not very steady shape of Charles. 'Bella, darling,' he said, kissing her on both cheeks. 'I've been looking all over for you. They ought to page people at this party. I wonder if you'd be terribly kind and give a word of advice to a young niece of mine. She's awfully keen to go on the stage and I thought, being such a star, you were the person to talk to.'

Bella got a slight satisfaction in seeing a look of annoyance flicker across Angora's face. She obviously felt she was the one who ought to be consulted.

'I'd love to,' said Bella and, without even saying goodbye to Steve, she followed Charles back into the crowd.

The stage-struck niece had a horse face and half Chelsea Flower Show on her head.

'It must be amazing to be acting at the Britannia,' she said. 'I suppose you pulled strings.'

'No,' said Bella, 'not even a tiny thread, but I had a lucky break. Have you had much experience?'

'No. I played Juliet in the school play. Everyone said I was awfully good.'

Oh God! Bella groaned inwardly. 'Have you tried to get into any of the drama schools?' she said.

'No. Perhaps you could give me a list of names. And perhaps you could introduce me to your director. I gather he's very charming.'

'Very,' said Bella. Her mind started to wander.

The horse-faced niece droned on and on.

'Incredible, fantastic, amazing,' said Bella at suitable intervals. Then she said, 'How marvellous'. The horse-faced girl looked at her in surprise.

'How marvellous,' said Bella again.

'I said Mummy was in Harrods when the bomb went off last week,' said the girl.

'Oh God, I'm sorry,' said Bella. 'I misheard you. There's such a din going on.'

Next moment one of Horseface's friends came up and they started shrieking at each other. Bella escaped, but not before she heard Horseface saying, 'That's Rupert's fiancée. I don't think she's quite all there.'

Bella retreated to a pillar again and ate three more éclairs, malevolently surveying the rest of the crowd.

'Don't look so horrified,' said a voice. 'You chose to marry into this lot.'

She jumped nervously. It was Lazlo.

'They're a load of junk,' she snapped. 'They should be driven over a cliff with pitch forks.'

Lazlo laughed. 'I'm glad you're enjoying yourself.'

A waitress came by with a tray.

'Have an ice,' he said. 'Children are supposed to like them, aren't they?'

'I hate ices,' her voice rose shrilly, 'more than anything else in the world except you.'

At that moment Teddy came up, looking distraught.

'Hullo, Bella,' he said. 'I say, Lazlo, I thought pregnant women only threw up in the morning. Gay's puking her guts out upstairs. I'm sure Constance is going to smell a rat. She wants us to cut the cake now. She's terrified everyone is going to drink too much.'

'Poor old Teddy,' said Lazlo, 'But you did go into this with your flies open.'

'I certainly did,' sighed Teddy. 'It's hell being a bridegroom. No one talks to you because they all think you ought to be talking to someone else.'

He wandered off, looking miserable, and they were immediately joined by a smooth looking man with auburn hair and heavy-lidded eyes.

'Lazlo!'

'Henri my dear, how are things?'

'Pretty rough. I've had to sell half my horses and I've had to sell off the land, but at least they've let me keep the shooting. Hope you'll come and stay for the twelfth.' He held out his glass to be filled by a passing waiter.

'I say,' he went on. 'Where's this chorus girl Rupert's got himself mixed up with. One hears such conflicting views. Charles is evidently rather smitten, but he always liked scrubbers. The rest of the family seem to think she's absolute hell.'

Bella went white.

'Judge for yourself,' said Lazlo. 'This is Bella.'

'Oh God,' said the red-headed man, looking not at all embarrassed. 'Trust me to put both feet in it.' He gave Bella a horse-flesh-judging once-over, then said, 'I must say I'm inclined to agree with Charles. You're bound to get opposition if you marry into this lot; they're so bloody cliquey. It'll be your turn next, Lazlo. One of those pretty girls you run around with will finally get her claws into you.'

'Hardly,' said Lazlo. 'Just because I enjoy a good gallop it doesn't necessarily mean I want to buy the horse.'

The red-headed man laughed.

'Cold-blooded sod aren't you? I must say you've got a pretty smart crowd here today. Aren't those a couple of Royals I see through the smoke?'

'My Aunt Constance,' said Lazlo, 'would get blue blood out of a stone. I suppose I'd better go and organize someone or we'll be here till midnight.'

Gay, looking pea-green but fairly composed, reappeared to cut the cake. Rupert fought his way over to Bella's side.

'God, what a hassle. The most terrible things are happening. Uncle Willy's just exposed himself to one of Teddy's female tenants. Has Lazlo been taking care of you?'

'I'm sure he'd like me taken care of,' said Bella.

Someone rapped the table. The speeches were mercifully short.

Lazlo stood up first to propose Gay's and Teddy's health. He was the sort of person who could quieten a room just by clearing his throat.

'I'm sorry,' he said, in his husky, slightly foreign voice, 'that so many of you have had to miss Goodwood. We all appreciate the sacrifice.' He then proceeded to read out the Goodwood results.

God, that laid them in the aisles. They were all in stitches.

'Bloody funny,' said Rupert.

In a corner Uncle Willy was so drunk he was trying to light an asparagus roll.

Lazlo then told a couple of jokes – Bella had to admire his timing – before raising his glass to Gay and Teddy. Everyone round her drained empty glasses. The drink, due to Constance's parsimony, was running short.

Teddy got up.

His heart was in his mouth, he said, and, as his old Nanny had told him never to talk with his mouth full, he'd better shut up. God, they fell about at that too. I wish I played to audiences like that, thought Bella.

He just wanted to thank Constance and Charles, he added, and toast the jolly pretty bridesmaids. The best man replied briefly and the room became a great twittering aviary again. Children were beginning to get over-excited and run through people's legs. Grandmothers retired to the sidelines to rest their swelling ankles. Suddenly, there was a loud bang on the table and Bella turned hearing Charles's voice.

'I won't keep you a moment,' he said, his voice slurring, his eyes glazed.

'Pissed as a newt as usual,' said someone behind Bella.

'I won't keep you a minute,' he said again. 'But I just wanted everyone to know how absolutely delighted Constance and I are that our son, Rupert, has just announced his engagement to a very talented and beautiful girl.'

'Charles,' thundered Constance, magenta with rage.

'Pissed as a newt,' said the voice again.

'I want you to drink to Bella and Rupert,' said Charles. 'I know she'll be an asset to us all.'

Half the marquee had started mumbling. 'Bella and Rupert,' when Chrissie suddenly said, very loudly, 'It's not true. She's not an asset. She's horrible, horrible. She's the biggest bitch that ever lived.'

There was a dreadful, embarrassed silence.

'Shut up, Chrissie,' snarled Rupert.

'What's that, what's that?' everyone was saying.

Lazlo had crossed the room in a flash.

'Come on, baby, that's enough. Upstairs with you.'

'You don't understand. No one understands anything,' said Chrissie and, wrenching her arms away from Lazlo, she fled out of the marquee.

Bella had also had enough. She fought her way out into the street and immediately found a taxi. Just as she had got in and was telling the driver to take her to the theatre, Rupert appeared at the window.

'Bella darling, please wait.'

'No, I will not,' she hissed. 'I've had enough of you and your bloody family for one afternoon. I'm not going to stand around getting insulted any more. Go on,' she said to the driver. 'Get going.'

'Darling,' pleaded Rupert, 'for Christ's sake let me explain.'

As the taxi moved off he reached in to grab her arm, but caught hold of the fox's tail instead, which promptly came off in his hand.

Bella leaned out of the car,

'And I'll report you to the R.S.P.C.A. for cruelty to foxes,' she screamed back at him.

CHAPTER EIGHT

SHE couldn't wait to get to the theatre to pour out all her miseries to Rosie Hassell.

When she arrived, she discovered Rosie was off with 'flu and an understudy was taking her place. The poor girl was absolutely sick with nerves and needed all the boosting Bella could give her.

Here I am at twenty-four, a real trouper with a Manx Fox, thought Bella, and she started to giggle helplessly. All the same, she gave a terrible performance. She couldn't concentrate and she kept drying up and fluffing her lines.

Rupert rang her in the interval. It took all his powers of persuasion to get her to come out that evening.

'Chrissie was tight,' he said. 'She's been on a diet, hasn't eaten properly for days, and she's got this sort of crush on me. She passed out when she got upstairs. She'll be absolutely mortified in the morning.'

'She's not coming out with us tonight?'

'I don't think so – just Angora, Steve, Lazlo and one of his birds.'

'The Heavy Brigade,' said Bella.

But she couldn't resist another chance to get at Steve.

She made a real hash of the last act. Wesley Barrington had to carry her the whole way. There was a great deal of applause at the end, both for him and the understudy.

'Roger's out front,' said Wesley, out of the corner of his mouth, as bowing and smiling, they took the last curtain call.

'Oh God,' said Bella. 'I'd better make myself scarce.'

Roger, however, came back-stage immediately.

'Well done,' he said to the understudy, his square freckled face breaking into a smile of approval. 'That was a lovely performance. Now clear out and get changed somewhere else.'

When she had gone, he shut the door and leant against it.

'That was a cock-up, wasn't it,' he said grimly. 'I suppose you got tight at the wedding.'

Bella shook her head. 'Not enough. That was the trouble.'

'Hell – was it?'

'Hell would seem like a day at the seaside compared with that little bunfight. The Henriques really don't like outsiders, do they? Trespassers are very much persecuted.'

She lit a cigarette with a trembling hand.

'Putting the heat on, are they? Are you sure you're doing the right thing, marrying this boy?'

'Oh, not you too,' groaned Bella. 'I thought you were my friend.'

'I am, and one of your greatest fans too. I know you can make it really big, but not if you go on giving lousy performances like this evening. You're in bad shape, angel. If I touched you, you'd twang. And you look frightful too. No one looking at you could see any reason why Othello should have the hots for you.'

'Thanks a lot,' said Bella, and started to laugh.

'That's better. Now you've got three days off, haven't you? For God's sake get some sleep. What are you going to do?'

'Spend the weekend at the Henriques' country hot seat.'

'You'll enjoy that. It's very plushy. Hot and cold servants in every bedroom, and the country is absolutely magical.'

'If that's supposed to cheer me up,' said Bella, 'it's an experience I would gladly forgo. You know how I hate the country.'

It was only when she got out of her costume that she realized she'd brought nothing to wear. She hated the willow green dress as she hated hell pains. The only alternative was a T-shirt with a picture of Clark Gable on the front and a crumpled pair of black knickerbockers which had been at the bottom of her cupboard for weeks and smelt of old mushrooms.

Oh well, she thought, tugging them on, I've got the top batting average for wearing the wrong clothes, why spoil the record?

It was four o'clock in the morning and the night had fallen to pieces around her. They had gone from disco to disco, and ended up in one of Rupert's haunts, where the musicians played cool jazz.

Chrissie had cried off, pleading a headache.

She can't stand seeing me and Rupert together, Bella thought wryly. And Lazlo had brought a ravishing Spanish girl with him, with a long black plait trailing down her beautiful brown back.

Steve had ignored Bella all evening. It was as though a sheet of glass had risen between them. Not once did he ask her to dance.

She was dead with exhaustion, but some masochistic streak wouldn't allow her to go home.

They were all dancing now, Steve still laughing with Angora. Rupert, his cheeks flushed, his hair tousled over his face like some Bacchante, was pressing his body against Bella's, muttering endearments into her ear. Lazlo was kissing his beautiful Spaniard, his hands slowly caressing her brown back, which was arched towards him in ecstatic submission, the two of them exuding so much white-hot sexuality it rubbed off on everyone else.

I can't stand it, thought Bella in agony, and wrenching herself away from Rupert, she fled into the loo and burst into a storm of weeping.

After a few minutes she managed to pull herself together and looked at her face in the mirror. It was pale grey. She rubbed some lipstick on to her cheeks. The effect was horrible.

And you can stop grinning too! she snarled silently at Clark Gable, who was baring his teeth across her bosom.

Rupert was dancing with the Spanish girl when she got back to the table. Lazlo was smoking a cigar. Bella sat down as far away from him as possible and gazed into her drink.

'You won't find the truth in the bottom of a shot of Johnnie Walker,' he said.

The light from an opening door suddenly lit up the long scar down the side of his face.

Curious, in spite of herself, Bella asked, 'Where did you get that scar?'

'In Buenos Aires. A man called Miguel Rodriguez pulled a knife on me.'

'What for?'

'He thought I was having it off with his wife.'

'What did you do?'

'I killed him!'

Bella shivered. 'But why?'

'He'd have killed me otherwise, and I was – er – quite fond of his wife.'

'There must have been a frightful scandal.'

'Frightful. But there have been worse since. People soon forget.'

She started to laugh scornfully but, somehow, the laugh got out of hand and went on and on.

'This isn't doing you any good, is it?' he said.

'I'm all right,' she snapped.

He picked up her hand and examined it. 'Maybe, but bitten nails do not denote serenity. The woods are deep and dark and full of tigers. You'd be very wise to pack Rupert in.'

'Over my dead body,' she hissed, snatching her hand away from him.

Then the inevitable happened. Steve and Angora were no longer there.

Lazlo gave Rupert and Bella a lift. The top of the car was down, the night all warm, and Bella looked up at the endless stars, trying to convince herself her life wasn't over.

Rupert put his arm round her.

'Don't maul me,' she yelled, suddenly at breaking point.

There was a shocked silence. Rupert went white. 'Take it easy, darling,' he said gently.

'I'm sorry, love,' said Bella, a moment later taking his hand.

But in the driving mirror, she saw a glint of satisfaction in Lazlo's eyes.

CHAPTER NINE

As a result of hangovers, none of them had gone down to the country until late on the day after Gay's wedding. They all felt jaded. The only answer seemed to start drinking again.

It was Angora, probably at Lazlo's instigation, who suggested they play table-turning. Everyone, except Bella, agreed with alacrity. A polished table and a glass were found; the lights were dimmed.

At first the glass produced no messages for anyone; then, chided by Chrissie that the spirits would not work unless they stopped fooling about, they started to concentrate.

The glass hovered a bit, then spelt out that Lazlo was going on a journey, which impressed everyone because he was flying to Zurich tomorrow night, and it told Angora she was due for measles.

Then it spelt Mabel.

'We don't know anyone called Mabel,' said Angora.

'Yes, we do,' said Steve. 'Bella, of course.'

'Bella?' said Rupert in surprise. 'But she's Isabella.'

'No, she's not. I've known her longer than you and her name's not Bella. She was born Mabel Figge, to be exact.'

Bella blushed scarlet.

Angora gave a crow of joy. 'You're never called Mabel Figge!' And she went off into peals of laughter. Chrissie grinned delightedly.

'Shut up, Angora!' snapped Rupert. 'Let's go on with the message for Bella.'

They all put their fingers on the glass.

'G-o h-o-m-e' it spelt out slowly. Then, suddenly, taking on a life of its own, it veered round the table, spelling out 'T-w-o t-i-m-i-n-g g-o-l-d d-i-g-g-e-r.'

There was a long pause.

Then Bella screamed, 'Someone's pushing that glass!'

'Darling,' Rupert protested, 'it's only a game.'

'And you can shut up!' she shouted at him, and, jumping to her feet, she caught her bag on the edge of the table. Everything cascaded on to the floor, her mirror breaking.

'And I hope it brings you all seven hundred years' bad luck!' she screamed.

She gave a sob and fled upstairs, locking herself in her bedroom and lying on her bed, crying just loudly enough for people to hear.

Later, Rupert came upstairs and banged on her door until she let him in.

'You're over-reacting,' he said. 'They're only teasing.'

'Throwing darts into a maddened bull, more likely,' she stormed.

He started kissing her; then followed the inevitable row because he wanted to make love to her. Suddenly, the fight went out of her.

'Oh well, go on if you must, I don't care,' she said listlessly.

Rupert stared at her for a minute.

'Thanks,' he said coldly, 'but I never accept charity,' and walked out of the room, slamming the door behind him.

It was early dawn when she finally fell asleep, and late dawn when she woke up, head splitting, gravel behind her eyes.

Desperate for aspirins, she got up and wandered down the passage to the bathroom she shared with Angora.

There were no pills in the cupboard, only bath salts and cologne. She weighed herself on the scales. God, she was putting on weight. She must stop all this misery eating.

She got off the scales and turned them up seven pounds. That would screw up Angora and her flaming slimming diets.

On the way back, she paused outside Angora's bedroom. The door was ajar. She peered in, uneasily breathing in the smell of French cigarettes, nail-polish and expensive scent. Then her nails bit into her palms as she realized there was no one sleeping in the bed. Angora must be with Steve. Until now, Bella had nurtured a faint hope he was just chasing Angora to goad her into breaking it off with Rupert.

Now she imagined his suntanned hands caressing Angora's body, her cloudy black hair on the pillow, her little gasps of excitement, her head threshing back and forth like a meningitis victim, as Steve drove her to the extremes of pleasure that Bella knew of old he was capable of. Then, later, the low laughter, the private jokes, the exchanged cigarettes, the sleeping in each other's arms.

She sat on her bed for a few minutes, whimpering. It was impossibly hot already.

She got up and opened the shutters and stepped out on to the balcony.

The fields were white with dew, a heavy mist hung over the lake at the bottom of the lawn. The white climbing roses on their tall arches were touched with pink. On the tennis court birds were chasing worms; in the distance a train chugged.

The beauty of the view only intensified her misery. A light breeze caressed her bare legs and lifted her hair off her shoulders.

Suddenly, she heard a scrunch of wheels and, leaning over the balcony, she saw the ivy green Mercedes draw up in front of the house. Lazlo got out. He was wearing a red and white striped shirt and dark grey trousers, and carrying his jacket and tie.

Bella stepped out of his line of vision, but, through a crack in the shutter, she watched him yawn and stretch, breathing in the morning air. Then, whistling, he set off across the dew-soaked lawn towards the stables.

The next moment, she heard a door shut quietly and saw Angora, wearing a white silk dressing gown, steal across the drive and then the lawn, after him. Then she called his name. He turned round, smiled and walked back towards her.

There was a quivering expectancy about Angora, as though she was longing for him to take her in his arms. For a minute they talked in low voices, with Bella nearly falling off the balcony in her efforts to hear. Then Lazlo picked up a loose strand of hair which had fallen over Angora's forehead and smoothed it behind her ear. She seemed to be arguing now; then he patted her cheek and nodded towards the direction of the house. Reluctantly she came running back across the grass and disappeared through the front door.

Bella opened her door slightly, but Angora didn't come back to her room. Had she gone to Steve's bedroom, or Lazlo's?

CHAPTER TEN

A BEAUTIFUL blazing day soared out of the mist. Bella lay by the swimming pool, trying to learn her lines. It was mid-morning. Out in the park, the sun touched the pale green shoulders of the elm trees, cattle grazed contentedly in the lush grass beside the lake, and Lazlo's two golden retrievers frolicked on the lawn.

It was impossible to imagine a view more serene, yet Bella felt sick with terror.

Anxious to avoid Rupert, she had got up early and gone to buy some aspirins at the local shop. She knew one of the fleet of servants would have provided them, but she wanted an excuse to get out of the house.

Just as she was leaving, a window box crashed from one of the balconies, missing her by inches.

The gardener, of course, was profuse in his apologies.

But twice later, as she wandered along the narrow country lanes, a large blue car roared past her, driving so close that she would have been run over if she hadn't leapt on to the verge.

Lazlo's behind this, she thought. He's capable of getting rid of Miguel Rodriguez because he'd got in his way; why not me too?

She tried to concentrate on learning her lines for *The Seagull.* She was playing Masha, the plain and ageing spinster, loved by the schoolmaster, but, in her turn, hopelessly in love with the son of the house. Every line she read seemed to parallel her own set-up:

'I am in mourning for my life, I am unhappy ... It isn't money that matters, a poor man may be happy ... Oh, nonsense, your love touches me but I cannot return it ... Help me, help me, or I shall do something silly. I shall make a mockery of my life and ruin it. I can't go on ... I am miserable. No one knows how miserable I am. I love Konstantin.'

She might have been speaking about her situation with Rupert and Steve. 'I shall make a mockery of my life and ruin it,' she repeated.

A shadow fell across her book. She jumped violently, then realized it was Steve.

It was the first time she'd been alone with him since that evening in the theatre. Even in the blazing sunshine he looked brown.

He was wearing navy blue bathing trunks and a pair of dark glasses, so she couldn't read the expression in his eyes as he looked down at her.

As always, she felt her stomach go liquid with desire.

'Hi stranger,' he said softly. 'May I talk with you?'

He sat down beside her.

'I don't know what game you're playing,' she blurted out.

'What game, honey? You tell me.'

'Telling me one moment you wanted me to break it off with Rupert because you were so crazy about me, then ignoring me the next. Sending me up. Telling the others my real name. Blatantly chatting up Angora just to hurt me.'

'I've been doing a little more than chatting up,' he said, pinching one of her cigarettes.

'Do you love her?'

'I don't understand words like love; they're not in my vocabulary, but she's extremely attractive. Let's say we enjoy each other.'

'Maybe you do,' said Bella steadily. 'But not enough to stop her slipping out at dawn to have a private confab with Lazlo.'

Just for a second Steve paused.

'How do you know?'

'I couldn't sleep. I opened my shutters. Lazlo came home about six, no doubt from shacking up with some of the local talent. Within ten seconds, Angora was out of the house. She'd obviously been waiting for him. They had some kind of hassle, then he persuaded her to come back into the house.'

Steve shrugged his shoulders. 'She's entitled to a commercial break if she wants one. The programme was good enough.'

'But don't you see,' Bella went on desperately, 'they're in

cahoots together. Angora's simply being manipulated by Lazlo. He's pulled off a marvellous film deal for her. She's very ambitious. He's probably been knocking her off as well, and, in return, she's agreed to lure you away from me. She's pretty formidable when she pulls out the stops. I defy anyone, even you, to resist her. And Lazlo knows what I feel about you. That seeing you and Angora together is driving me round the twist. That it's the one thing that'll make me break it off with Rupert.'

Steve yawned so hard he nearly dislocated his jaw.

'You always had too much imagination,' he said. 'And keep your trap shut, the others are coming. Hi Chrissie. Hi Rupe. The midges are terrible. You'd better come up and see my itchings sometime.'

Bella flopped down on her lilo in despair.

Rupert sat down beside her. Even on the hottest day of the year, he still had the look of a hothouse plant exposed to a killing draught. He was wearing a black shirt with the collar turned up, as if against some imagined storm, and looked at Bella with bruised, troubled eyes, and eyelids swollen from lack of sleep.

How he'd changed from the cool, bitchy self-confident little boy she'd met six months ago.

She put out her hand to stroke his face. He imprisoned it and held it against his cheek.

'Oh, darling, we must stop fighting. I can't stand another night like last night.'

I can't go on torturing him much longer, she thought unhappily. I must break it off with him, but not yet. I'm not going to give Lazlo the satisfaction of thinking he directly engineered it.

Chrissie, very white, and too fat for her scarlet bikini, sat down under an umbrella, and started the *Daily Mail* crossword.

Steve dived into the pool, his muscular arms coming out of the bright turquoise water as he did a leisurely crawl to the other side.

'It's lovely once you get in,' he called to Chrissie.

And eventually, after a lot of badinage, he persuaded her to join him in the water, where he chased her round the pool, tickling her, diving for her ankles, making her shriek with laughter and fear.

Rupert edged away as a particularly violent piece of splashing soaked his shirt.

'I detest horseplay,' he said. 'And I don't feel much more kindly towards Mr. Benedict.'

Giggling frantically, Chrissie clambered out of the pool and ran along the edge to take refuge under the umbrella. Steve picked up a towel and, catching up, began to dry her, laughing down at her, his eyelashes stuck together with water, his blue eyes rivalling the drained sapphire of the sky. Gradually, in his arms, she calmed down and stopped giggling.

'I'm going to oil you,' he said. 'And you're going to lie in the sun and stop hiding your very considerable lights under a bushel.'

'I'll oil her,' said Rupert sharply, getting to his feet and almost snatching the bottle of Ambre Solaire from Steve.

Bella felt a stab of guilt as she saw the ecstasy in Chrissie's face as Rupert rubbed it into her back.

She returned to her lines, little red spots leaping in front of her eyes.

'*Oh nonsense*,' she whispered. '*Your love touches me but I cannot return it*.'

'What's the largest organ in the body, five letters?' said Chrissie.

'Penis,' said Angora, drifting towards them in her white silk dressing-gown, carrying a photograph album, a cigarette dangling from her scarlet lips.

Chrissie giggled. 'It can't be. Did you sleep well?'

'I didn't do much sleeping, thank you, darling. But I had a lovely night.'

'You made a bloody awful din,' said Rupert.

'Steve likes to hear the sound of his own vice,' said Angora, dropping a kiss on Steve's shoulder.

Steve's eyes met Bella's. See! his triumphant expression seemed to be saying.

Angora lay down on a lilo, stretching out her scarlet painted toes, admiring her sleek brown legs. Her almost Japanese slenderness always made Bella feel like a carthorse.

'Hullo, Belladonna,' she said. 'You look a bit peaky, darling.

Shouldn't go to bed so early. What you need is a few late nights.'

Bella ignored her.

'I can't go on,' she repeated in a whisper. *'I'm miserable, no one knows how miserable. I love Konstantin.'*

'Who?' said Angora. 'Oh, I see, you're learning lines. You are virtuous. I haven't had a script from Harry Backhaus yet, and we start shooting next week sometime. I gather the costumes are heaven. I do hope I'm not expected to take mine off. The set always gets so crowded.'

God, she's hell! thought Bella. How can Chrissie look at her with such admiration.

'Don't you get tired of people asking you to be sexy all the time?' said Chrissie.

'They don't have to ask,' said Steve, lobbing a pebble on to Angora's back.

'Well it's not something I mind,' said Angora, 'like being bitten by midges. Steve, darling, do light another fag and drive them away. Now I want you all to gather round and look at this photograph album.'

'Is it yours?' said Chrissie.

'No – yours, but guess who keeps cropping up in it.'

She flicked a few pages.

'There's Rupert. Wasn't he an adorable baby? And there's Chrissie on a pony, and Gay at her first teenage party. It was the Hunter-Blake's firework party. And look who's over there.'

'My God! It's you,' said Steve.

'Wasn't I awful? Only fourteen then and still a virgin. Look who couldn't wait for it.'

Steve examined the photograph more closely:

'You weren't that bad. I wish I'd been around at the time. I'd have sorted you out.'

Angora turned over another page. 'There's Lazlo; not so hot in those days was he? Bit thin and beaky-nosed. And look, there's Constance getting her O.B.E.

'And there I am at fifteen, at the Bullingdon Point to Point, not a virgin any more. Look a lot happier, don't I? I was wearing falsies, although you wouldn't know it under all that heather-mixture tweed. And there's the guy who did it, Jamie Milbank. He's married with three children now.'

'Jamie Milbank!' said Chrissie, 'but he's so respectable.'

'I was his final fling. And there I am again, at Gay's coming-out dance. Isn't it amazing how one crops up in other people's photograph albums?'

I never do, thought Bella wistfully. Once more she felt miserably conscious of being out of it.

'There's Lazlo again,' said Angora. 'Looking much more glamorous now, and there he is with a bird. And there's Rupert making a duck in the Eton and Harrow match. You look disgustingly pleased, Rupe darling. I suppose you were dying to get back to the bar.

'There's Lazlo with yet another bird. What's so extraordinary is he and I never met until this year.'

Steve looked at the photograph and whistled. 'Some chick. How does he manage to get all those broads?'

Angora giggled. 'Well, I'm only going by hearsay darling, but they tell me he's the fastest tongue in the West.'

Everyone howled with laughter until a dry voice behind them said, 'You talk too much, Angora.'

It was Lazlo, wearing dark glasses and black bathing trunks. He was carrying the morning papers and a large drink.

'What are you drinking?' said Chrissie.

'It says whisky on the bottle.'

'At this hour?' said Angora in mock horror.

'It says so all the time,' said Lazlo.

'You'll ruin your looks that way,' said Angora.

'Very probably,' said Lazlo. And sitting down on the edge of the pool, he turned to the racing pages.

Bella had to admit, reluctantly, that he was in extremely good shape.

She was pouring with sweat. She longed to swim, but it would make her hair even more fluffy than ever, and she was damned if she was going to ask Chrissie or Angora if she could borrow their rollers.

'How many horses have you got running this afternoon?' said Steve.

'Two,' said Lazlo. '*The Times* seems to think one of them's going to win.'

'You know Isidore, who fixes everyone's divorces,' said

Angora. 'He's sold all his horses, he's so terrified of the wealth tax.'

'Any minute now,' said Lazlo, 'the man in the street's going to go into the betting shop and find there aren't any horses to bet on.'

It was too hot – to hell with her hair. She got up and walked to the edge of the pool.

Conscious suddenly of the highly charged atmosphere, she tried to dive in gracefully, but promptly did a belly flop.

As she swam up and down, she was aware of Lazlo's sardonic, appraising eyes watching her, looking for chinks in her armour, presumably wondering, like the chief torturer in the Spanish Inquisition, what refinement to try next.

I'll end up with my feet in cement at the bottom of this pool if I stay here much longer, she thought.

She got out and dried herself and looked round for her script. Lazlo was reading it.

'*Your love touches me, but I can't reciprocate it. Help me, or I shall do something silly.*' He read softly, so only she could hear.

'Can I have it back, please?' snapped Bella.

'Of course. Do you realize now how much better you'll play Masha than Nina?'

Bella's yellow eyes narrowed.

'So you *were* behind that little chess move,' she said.

'Naturally,' he said. 'Why don't you admit you've had enough?'

'I bloody well won't.'

'That's a nice ring,' he said admiring the gold band studded with seed pearls on her little finger. 'Where did you get it from?'

'Rupert gave it to me,' she said.

'I might have known it,' he sighed. 'It's the only jewellery in remotely decent taste I've ever seen you wear. Although,' his eyes travelled over her body, 'I must confess in a bikini you look more chic than I've ever seen you.'

Angora, who disliked anyone's attention to be off her for very long, started reading out the horoscopes in the paper. 'What are you, Lazlo?' she said.

'Scorpio,' said Chrissie.

'Oh very passionate,' said Angora. 'Ruled by the privates.'

Everyone laughed. 'It says you're going to have a tricky weekend, so play things close to the chest. What's Bella?'

'Taurus,' said Rupert.

'Um,' Angora's eyes ran down the page. 'People around you just aren't too co-operative, but be prepared to stick to your guns and argue things out.'

Bella looked up, met Lazlo's eyes, flushed and looked away again.

'And now Rupert, what's he?'

'Aquarius,' said Chrissie promptly. She knew at once, thought Bella, and I haven't a clue.

'Oh dear,' sighed Angora. 'What a pity you've decided to marry Bella. Taurus and Aquarius are terrible together. You've got an awfully stormy marriage ahead, darling. You'd better think twice about it.'

'So you keep telling us, Angora,' said Rupert angrily. 'Would you bloody well mind getting off our backs?'

'Go and get ready, Angora,' said Lazlo. 'I know you're governed by double summer time, but unless you get moving, we'll be two hours late for the first race.'

He got up and dived into the water. Bella experienced the same surprise that she would have felt seeing a big cat allowing itself to get wet.

CHAPTER ELEVEN

BELLA was not on any sort of terms with Chrissie or Angora to ask them what was worn at Goodwood. It was far too hot to wear stockings, and her legs weren't brown enough to go without, but it seemed stupid to waste the sun, so she put on a pair of dungarees in dark blue denim, superbly cut to show off her long legs. She wore nothing else on top. The straps and bib made a pretty good job of covering her breasts if she didn't leap about too much.

Of course, she was the last out. They were all standing beside the Mercedes, like some magnificent five: Chrissie and Angora both in pretty flowery dresses, Rupert and Steve in lightweight suits. Lazlo, however, in an impeccably cut pinstripe suit with a dark red carnation in the buttonhole, made everyone else look sloppy by comparison.

He laughed when he saw Bella. 'Have you come to mend the boiler?' he said.

Steve and Angora sat in the front beside Lazlo. To make more room, Steve sat slightly sideways, his arm along the back of the seat, his elbow resting against Angora's hair. His hand lay just in front of Bella and she had to resist a constant temptation to touch it.

Angora adjusted her hat in the driving mirror. 'Do you think I ought to cut my hair, Lazlo?' she said.

'No,' said Lazlo. 'I hate short hair.'

Life is just a bowl of cherries, Bella sighed, until you break your teeth on the stones.

She was turned on by the whole ambience of the racecourse, the heavy smell of hot horse, leather and dung, the shrill neighing from the stables.

She was surprised how done up everyone was. The women, very upper class, displaying thoroughbred ankles. The men were even better looking. The members' enclosure was crammed with Yock Yocks in light checked suits, with the kind of curly brimmed hats you put in rollers every night.

Bella found she got some pretty odd glances, and some wolf whistles too. It gave her considerable satisfaction that people were gazing at her more than Angora, and that two people came up and asked her for her autograph.

'We saw you on television the other day. We thought you were so good.'

That annoyed Angora too.

In the paddock, the horses were circling for the first race.

Bella admired their scarlet nostrils, rolling eyes and impossibly fragile legs, and realized how exactly right the artists had drawn them in those old sporting prints.

'That's Lazlo's horse, Chaperone, over there,' said Rupert, pointing to a chestnut, gleaming like a furniture polish advertisement. 'She looks well, doesn't she?'

'Beautiful,' sighed Bella, as the filly walked by, nuzzling at her groom, proudly flaunting the green and black rug, with the initials L.C.H. on the corner.

'She's the only one who's walking out,' said Steve approvingly.

Who with? wondered Bella.

Out came the jockeys. How tiny they looked with their shrill voices and Jack Russell jauntiness.

Lazlo went into the paddock. Trainers, owners and jockeys stood in isolated islands, discussing last minute tactics, the trainers telling jokes and making reassuring noises to the jockeys, like the bride's father before the trip up the aisle.

'Will the jockeys mount please,' said the loudspeaker.

Chaperone was led in. She dropped her head on Lazlo's shoulder in a friendly fashion, leaving a large smear of green froth on his suit.

'I must go and wish him luck,' said Angora, about to duck under the rails.

'I wouldn't,' said Rupert. 'He's busy. Racing's the only thing he takes really seriously.'

Apart from getting rid of me, thought Bella.

'That's Lazlo's jockey, Charlie Lamas, getting up now,' Rupert went on. 'Lazlo brought him over from South America.'

Bella watched the little man with a leathery face and mournful dark eyes being hoisted up on to Chaperone's back. He swore at her, as she gave two light-hearted bucks, and sent her clattering down the tarmac after the other horses.

'Just time to place our bets,' said Rupert, taking Bella's arm.

They all backed Chaperone, except Bella who, out of sheer cussedness, backed an outsider, Hera's Pride.

From the members' stand they could see the heat haze shimmering on the rails, as the horses cantered down to the start.

Down below them, rumour and speculation seethed, cauldron-like round the bookies, with their knowing, magenta faces. The tic-tac men gesticulated frantically.

A minute before the start, Lazlo joined the party, looking louche and piratical, and chewing on his cigar.

'Good luck,' said Angora.

'They're under starter's orders,' said Rupert, raising his binoculars.

'They're orf,' said the loudspeaker.

Bella found herself watching Lazlo, rather than the race.

She had to admire his sang-froid as the field rocketed up the centre of the course, like mercury up a thermometer plunged into boiling water.

His hands clenched slightly on his binoculars. He puffed slightly faster on his cigar as he watched the filly flare promisingly into the lead for an instant, then slip to the back of the field as they streamed past the post.

There were no histrionics, no effing and blinding. He just moved away from the cries of sympathy that showered down on him, unable to speak for a minute from disappointment.

'Who won?' asked Bella, a minute later.

'Hera's Pride,' said Steve. 'I can't imagine anyone backing it.'

'I did,' said Bella. 'To my mind she was the only one who was walking out,' and, laughing in his face, she skipped down the steps to collect her winnings.

Her euphoria was short-lived. She lost a fiver on each of the next two races.

The high event of the day was the ladies' race, sponsored by the Bond Street jewellers who make those diamond brooches with ruby conjunctivitis, which rear up on smart racing women's lapels.

'Let's go and look at the gels,' leered a whiskery old gentleman with a purple face.

'Lazlo's got a horse in this race called Baudelaire,' said Rupert. 'It's a bit green, but Lazlo's got very high hopes for it. It's the black colt over there. He bought it in Ireland. They think black horses are unlucky there, so he got it cheap.'

Baudelaire, rolling his eyes wickedly, and snorting, marched round the paddock, snatching at his bit.

'They've had a devil of a problem getting weight on him,' said Rupert. 'He won't sleep; walks his box all night.'

'Sounds rather like his master,' said Angora.

Out came the women jockeys, one tall girl with blonde hair and very green eyes, the rest small and very slight. Binoculars were immediately focused on the transparent breeches which clung to the girls' svelte figures in the heat.

Chrissie looked at them enviously.

'Lazlo says if I lose two stone, he'll buy me a racehorse,' she said.

'Which is Lazlo's jockey?' said Steve.

'The prettiest one, of course,' said Chrissie. 'The tall one with green eyes.'

'Do you think he's banged her yet?' said Rupert.

Angora's eyes narrowed for a second, then she said lightly, 'If he hasn't, it won't be long.'

The start was in a different place this time, but Bella was determined to place her bet with the same bookie on the other side of the track.

'I'll meet you in the members' enclosure,' she called to Rupert.

'Bella, wait, you'll get lost,' he shouted after her.

She was returning across the course when, just as she reached the white railings, she realized she'd dropped her betting slip.

Turning, she saw it lying in the middle of the course. Without looking to left or right, she ran back to get it.

Suddenly there was a thundering in her ears and the ten

runners had come out of a side gate and were galloping towards her down to the start.

Terrified, she stood frozen to the spot, then tried to run back to the rails, but it was too late; they were on top of her. She screamed. They must crush her to death. Then, miraculously, Lazlo's black horse had swerved frantically to the right to avoid her, depositing his blonde rider on the grass, and galloping off down to the start.

The next moment Lazlo was picking her up. She'd never seen him so blazing angry before.

'What the fucking hell do you think you're doing? Trying to sabotage my horse?'

'What the hell are you doing, trying to kill me?' jibbered Bella. 'She was riding straight at me, no doubt at your instructions, and if it hadn't been for that darling horse swerving out of the way, I'd be a dead duck now.'

'Don't be bloody fatuous,' said Lazlo. 'Get off the course.'

He went over to pick up the blonde, who had staggered to her feet, shocked but unhurt.

Baudelaire, having shed his rider, was now having a high old time. Black tail straight up in the air, reins trailing on the ground, he cantered round the course, using up valuable energy.

To the delight of the crowd, and the shredded nerves of Lazlo, the stable lad and his blonde rider, he resolutely refused to be caught.

Rupert fought through the crowd to Bella's side.

'Darling, are you all right?'

'Of course I am. I just dropped my betting slip and your dear cousin's jockey rode straight at me.'

'She couldn't do much else,' said Rupert. 'They haven't got very good brakes, these horses.'

'He's doing marvellously now,' said Bella admiringly, watching Baudelaire scampering away from a couple of stewards and come cantering back down the course. 'He's got real star quality.'

'He's going to trip over the reins. They've got legs of glass, these horses,' said Rupert in anguish.

At last, after ten minutes cavorting, Baudelaire got bored and came to a violent, slithering halt in front of Lazlo, uttered a long, rolling snort through flared nostrils, and started eating grass.

The blonde girl was put up again. Rupert, Lazlo and Bella went back to the stands to watch the race.

'Hasn't got a hope in hell now,' said Lazlo angrily.

They were off, and for Bella it was the same old rat race. Listening to the whisper of 'Here they come, here they come' growing into a great roar, not being able to recognize any of the horses in the shifting kaleidoscope of colours.

'My God,' said Rupert, 'she's going to do it.'

And suddenly the tall blonde, crouched over Baudelaire's ears like a Valkyrie, by sheer force of personality and leg muscle, seemed to shake off the rest of the field and drive the black horse first past the post.

The stand erupted in excitement.

'Christ, what a finish. What a turn-up for the books,' said Rupert.

Back in the winner's enclosure, a great cheer went up as Baudelaire came in.

The blonde girl looked as cool as a cucumber; the other girls dripped with sweat, puce in the face, their mascara running as though they'd just come out of the sauna.

Baudelaire, his coat covered with the kind of subdued lather you get after the first application of shampoo, marched round the enclosure, still rolling his eyes and laughing in his equine way. Congratulations were being showered on Lazlo like confetti.

CHAPTER TWELVE

A GREAT deal of champagne was drunk after that, and Bella got separated from Rupert, and was eventually driven back home by a lot of Lazlo's racing cronies.

Chrissie, who'd come back with Rupert, had changed for dinner by the time Bella arrived. She looked prettier than Bella had ever seen her, wearing black, with a huge diamond glowing between her breasts.

'That's gorgeous,' said Bella, hoping to conciliate her, and picked up the diamond between finger and thumb.

'It's called the Evening Star,' said Chrissie, ignoring Bella and speaking directly to Angora. 'It's one of the most famous diamonds in the world. My mother would have a fit if she knew I was wearing it.'

Dinner finished, everyone discussed what to do next.

'We could play sardines,' said Angora. 'Or why not murder? I haven't played that since I was a child.'

'When was that?' said Steve. 'Yesterday?'

Angora pulled a face at him.

Lazlo looked at his watch. 'I've got to leave for the airport in an hour,' he said.

'Never mind,' said Chrissie, looking really excited for the first time in days. 'We can play a couple of rounds before you go.'

Oh no, thought Bella, not another of their horrible tribal games.

Angora dealt out the cards.

'Good.' Lazlo waved the King of Spades. 'I'm the detective. I can stay down here and drink brandy.'

'Wait till we get upstairs, Lazlo,' said Chrissie. 'Then turn the lights off at the main. We must do it properly.'

'I don't want to play,' said Bella quickly.

'Come on, don't be a spoilsport,' said Angora, taking her arm.

'Well, I'm going to stay with Rupert then.'

'No, you're not,' said Angora relentlessly as they climbed the main staircase. 'You go along that passage, Bella. Rupert go this way, and the rest of us will fan out towards the West Wing.'

As soon as she was alone, Bella quickened her pace. If she could find some room and lock herself in, she'd be safe.

She started to run, then, suddenly, everything was plunged into suffocating darkness as the lights went out. She fell over a chair, then found a door. It was locked. Whimpering with terror, she crossed the passage and found another door. That was locked, too.

Then she heard footsteps behind her – slow, relentless. She gave a sob. Slimy terror gripped her. She crashed across the passage again, found another door. It was open.

She shot inside and pulled it shut behind her. But there was no lock. Her heart pounding, she leant against it.

The footsteps grew closer, then stopped outside. Panic-stricken, she bolted across the room, crashing into more furniture, trying to find the window. Then she heard someone stealthily opening the door, then, equally stealthily, closing it. Someone was in the room with her.

'Who is it?' she croaked in terror.

Then, suddenly, as a waft of scent reached her, she nearly fainted with relief. She'd recognize that smell anywhere. It was Steve's aftershave.

'Steve!' she sobbed. 'Oh, Steve!'

'Are you by yourself?' came the whisper.

'Yes. I'm so frightened!'

She stumbled forward and, the next moment, she was in his arms and bursting into a flood of tears.

'I can't bear it! I can't bear it! Stop torturing me like this!'

He kissed her as he'd never kissed her before – as though he wanted to devour her and overwhelm her with the force of his passion. He must love her to kiss her like that.

'Why have you been so horrible to me?' she moaned, when she could speak.

'I had to make you come to heel. You can't marry Rupert. You know that.'

'Yes! Yes!'

'Promise you'll speak to him this evening?'

'I promise! Anything, anything. Just kiss me again.'

He pulled her down on to the bed. They erupted against each other.

'I want you,' he whispered. 'I want you – now.'

Any moment he'd be raping her and she didn't care.

It was a few seconds before they realized someone was screaming horribly.

'Bloody hell! Someone seems to have been murdered,' he said.

'Don't go! Don't leave me!'

He started to kiss her again, but the screaming went on, echoing unearthily through the house

'I'd better go and see what's going on. I'll sort you out later, but not until you've packed it in with Rupert.' And he was gone.

When the lights came on she realized she was in a strange bedroom, probably belonging to one of the maids. In a daze of happiness, she re-did her face and staggered downstairs. Steve loved her! She wasn't looking forward to breaking it off with Rupert, but it was no good marrying him if she really loved Steve.

She felt so free, she wanted to swing from the chandeliers.

Downstairs she found everyone standing round Chrissie, who was in hysterics

'It's gone!' she screamed 'It's gone!'

'What's gone?' said Lazlo sharply. 'Pull yourself together!'

'The Evening Star. I was upstairs. Someone put their hands round my neck and the next moment the diamond was gone. Oh! What will Mummy say?'

Bust a gut, thought Bella, and winked at Steve. But he didn't smile. He looked the picture of concern.

'Don't panic. I guess someone's playing a joke.'

'Bloody silly joke, whoever's playing it!' snapped Lazlo

'I'm going to call the police,' said Chrissie.

'Don't be crazy,' said Lazlo. 'Come on, let's look for it.'

But although they searched all the passages and rooms, no one could find any trace of the stone.

Lazlo looked at his watch. 'I've got to catch that plane. I must go. I'll ring you tomorrow,' he said, as he kissed Chrissie. 'And whatever you do, don't get the police in.'

And that, thought Bella, looking at Lazlo's broad departing back, is the last I'll ever see of that snake.

'I'm going to call Aunt Constance,' said Chrissie, going upstairs. But when she came back, ten minutes later, her eyes were glittering. 'I've rung the police,' she said defiantly. 'They'll be round any moment.'

Rupert frowned. 'That's a bit extreme, isn't it?'

Angora giggled. 'How exciting,' she said, starting to re-paint her lips a brilliant scarlet. 'Do you think they'll search me?'

'Sure to,' said Steve, rumpling her hair.

They smiled into each other's eyes.

Can't he let up even now, thought Bella; then she relented. Let him have his little game of taunting her; he'd be hers as soon as she broke it off with Rupert.

All the same, she felt twitchy. She hated the police. She hoped they wouldn't ask too many awkward questions. If they found out about her background, they might suspect her. Thank goodness she'd been with Steve all the time, and had a proper alibi.

When the police arrived, Chrissie talked to them first, then Steve, who stayed in there a long time, then Angora, Rupert, Lazlo's various racing cronies and, finally, Bella.

The C.I.D. man had a smooth, pink, deceptively homely face. After a few enquiries, he said politely. 'Your real name's Mabel Figge, isn't it, Miss Parkinson?'

She caught her breath. 'Yes – yes, that's right.'

'And your father died in prison, doing time for murder and robbery.'

'Yes.' She clasped her hands together to stop them from shaking.

After a few more questions it was quite obvious they knew all the appalling details of her past.

Who could have told them? Steve? No. Steve loved her. It must have been Angora or Chrissie, probably clued up by Lazlo.

'Where were you when the theft took place?'

Now she was on safe ground. 'I went up the main staircase and turned left towards the servants' quarters, and slipped into a room along that passage. Mr. Benedict followed me.' She blushed under the detective's scrutiny. 'We – er – spent the rest of the time together.'

'That's odd. Mr. Benedict says he was with Miss Fairfax, all the time, and she bears this out.'

Bella gave a gasp of horror. 'He's lying! He was with me.'

'He claims he was with Miss Fairfax in Miss Fairfax's bedroom. There was a lot of Miss Fairfax's lipstick on the shirt he was wearing.'

'It must be mine!'

'You don't wear bright scarlet lipstick, Miss Parkinson.'

'He's lying!' her voice rose.

'I've also got to warn you Miss Henriques claims that the person who put their hands round her neck and stole the diamond wore bracelets that jangled.' He looked at the three heavy gold rings on Bella's wrist.

'But that's absurd! Other people were wearing bracelets.'

'Not ones that jangled.'

'She's trying to frame me,' Bella whispered. 'She's madly in love with Rupert and he's engaged to me. They all hate me! They'd kill me rather than let me marry their darling Rupert. Oh, God!' She clasped her clenched fists to her mouth. She was badly out of control, on the verge of tears.

The pink-faced detective looked at her. Then, to her amazement, he said, 'All right, Miss Parkinson, you can go now.'

It was two o'clock in the morning, but she still made Rupert drive her straight back to London. She couldn't bear another moment under that roof. She didn't know what Steve was up to, but she knew the only way to get the Furies off her back was to break it off with Rupert.

As they were driving down the Bayswater Road, she took a deep breath and said, 'I'm sorry, Rupert. I know this sounds totally ridiculous and insane, but I can't marry you. I really can't. I'm afraid I'm in love with someone else.'

She had no idea how he took this because she was staring down at her hands.

'How long have you known this other chap?'

'Ages – but, well, he only came back into my life about a fortnight ago – the night, in fact, I was late for dinner, the first time I met your parents, I was with him.'

'And you still felt it was all right to get engaged to me?'

'I thought what I felt for you was the real thing, and that I was just infatuated by him, but now I know I can't live without him. I don't like him very much, but it's driving me out of my mind! I'm sorry, darling, I've not been thinking of you at all. I know I've been a bitch. I just thought I might grow to love you . . .' Her voice ran out in a thin line of drivel.

The car slowed down outside her flat. The pale green trees were lit up by the street lamps. Rupert looked quite calm, but he was as white as a sheet.

'We'd better talk about it upstairs.'

Outside Bella's flat, however, stood two men. 'Miss Parkinson?' said one of them.

'Yes!' snapped Bella. 'What do you want?'

'We're police officers, sir. We have a warrant to search Miss Parkinson's luggage.'

'Don't be bloody stupid!' said Rupert.

'It's all right,' said Bella. 'There's nothing in there. You're quite welcome to search it.'

But in the pocket of the smaller suitcase, wrapped in one of Bella's petticoats, they discovered the Evening Star.

'Someone put it there!' Bella screamed. 'I've been framed! I didn't take it!'

'I'm sorry, Miss Parkinson,' said the policeman imperturbably. 'I'm afraid we'll have to take you into custody.'

CHAPTER THIRTEEN

BELLA, when she looked back later, could recall very little about her spell in prison. She remembered Rupert making the most appalling scene when the police arrested her and, later, beating her fists against the door of her cell. She remembered appearing in court the following morning, nearly fainting with horror when the magistrate refused her bail, and finally being gripped by hysterical panic at finding herself locked in a cell in Holloway.

One of the wardresses had brought her some revolting stew, and a sardonic doctor with rimless glasses had asked her endless questions about herself. Afterwards, she lay on a hard, narrow bed trying to control her mounting desperation. Why had Steve denied being with her during the murder game? Who had betrayed her to the police? Was it Chrissie, Angora or Steve? Who had planted the diamond in her suitcase? Would the papers get all the details of her past? If they did, her career was finished. At intervals, the thought of Lazlo rose, black and churning, choking her like a wave of nausea. He's behind this, she thought, he's the one who cooked my goose.

I'm innocent, she said over and over again but, in spite of the stifling heat in the cell, she couldn't stop shivering.

Then a key turned in the door.

'The Prison Governor wants to see you,' said the wardress.

The Prison Governor had a kind, sheep-like face. She looked embarrassed. For a minute she played with a paper knife.

Then she said, 'I'm afraid there's been a mistake. The evidence was very conclusive against you, but the police have now discovered you've been framed. The Henriques family have withdrawn all charges.

'We're very sorry for all the worry this has caused you,' said the Prison Governor, flashing her big teeth. 'But of course, all the papers will print the fact that you're innocent. It'll be wonderful publicity.'

Bella didn't smile back.

'Why wasn't I allowed bail?'

'There have been several big diamond raids in the past few weeks. Police suspect the same gang at work. For some reason they felt you were mixed up in it.'

'Have they arrested anyone else?'

'Not yet.'

Suddenly she couldn't stand the awful sheep-like face any longer.

'I want to get out of here – at once.'

'Of course. There's a car waiting to take you to the Court, where you'll be released immediately.'

When she came out of court an hour later and felt the hot sun on her face, she threw back her head and took a deep breath. Then a group of reporters surged forward and started to bombard her with questions. Oh God! She hadn't thought they'd get on to the story so fast. Suddenly, a tall man in dark glasses grabbed her arm and pulled her down the steps into a waiting car. It was only after he'd driven off, leaving the reporters gaping, that she realized it was Lazlo Henriques.

'What the hell are you doing here?' she stormed. 'You're the last person I want to see. I thought you were in Zurich.'

'I was. Rupert rang me in hysterics this morning, begging me to come back and spring you from prison. The things I do for my family.'

'It was your rotten family who got me shut up in the first place.'

She was overcome by a terrible fit of shaking. Lazlo got out a packet of cigarettes, lit one, and handed it to her.

'Thanks,' she said, trying to get a grip on herself. 'Where's Rupert?'

'Gone to Zurich. Carrying on the deal I started. I thought it better if he was out of the way for a bit.'

'Just in case I might have second thoughts about getting re-engaged to him.'

Lazlo grinned. 'How perceptive you are, my dear.'

'Was it splashed all over the papers? My arrest?'

'It was too late for the dailies. But the evenings lead on it, with lots of pictures. By the final editions they'll be leading on your release. It'll look like a publicity stunt.'

'That's what the Prison Governor said.'

She started to relax. London in the blue haze of the late afternoon had never looked so lovely.

'Where are we going?' she asked.

'To my flat.'

'I want to go home.'

'Don't be silly. Once the big Press boys get on to this, they'll never leave you alone.'

'How did you manage to spring me, anyway?'

'Pulled a few strings, leaned on a few people.'

'I'd forgotten you were so influential. Who planted the diamond in my case?'

'I'll tell you the whole story when we get home.'

Lazlo's flat was a surprise. She had expected it to be as ugly and impersonal as the Henriques' London house. But it was sybaritic in the extreme, with grey silk walls, long fur rugs on the ground and brilliant scarlet curtains. Thousands of books and paintings covered the walls. Three large cats wandered up to welcome them.

Lazlo went straight to the drinks tray and poured Bella a vast brandy.

'Get that inside you.'

'I'm sorry, I'm still a bit stunned,' Bella said, taking the glass. 'Would you mind awfully if I had a bath?'

She soaked in emerald green scented water for a long time, and scrubbed and scrubbed herself to get every speck of prison dirt off. Later she pinched some of Lazlo's scent from the row of bottles near the bath. Odd that he used Black Opal like Steve.

She put on a dark green towelling dressing-gown that was hanging on the back of the door. In the kitchen she found Lazlo eating smoked salmon sandwiches and reading his mail.

'I've just weighed myself,' she said. 'I've lost five pounds in the last two days.'

Lazlo handed her the plate of sandwiches.

'Well, you'd better eat something. I'll get you another drink.'

'I'm not hungry,' she said. Then, realizing suddenly that she was ravenous, she wolfed the lot. The brandy was giving her heartburn, but a mild euphoria stole down inside her. She sat down on the sofa. A large ginger cat jumped on to her knee, and started purring and kneading her with his paws.

'How did you get me out?' she said.

'I told you, I leant on a few people.'

'But, *please*, who put the diamond in my case?'

A guarded look descended like a curtain over his face.

'Chrissie,' he said.

'Chrissie!' said Bella in amazement. 'What on earth for? It was *her* diamond.'

'She loves Rupert – to distraction. Seeing you and him together, when she knew you weren't in love with him, pushed her over the top. She thought – quite wrongly, as it turns out – that if you were arrested, Rupert would go off you.'

Bella thought for a minute. She'd gone through enough hell over Steve to understand exactly what Chrissie must have suffered.

'Oh poor, poor Chrissie,' she whispered.

For once Lazlo looked surprised. 'Well, it's nice of you to take it like that. The irony was that you broke it off with Rupert that evening anyway, so she needn't have bothered.'

'Did you tell the police she did it?'

He shook his head.

'How did you get me off then?'

'I said you were with someone else the whole time we were playing murder.'

Happiness flooded over her.

'Oh, so Steve's at last admitted that he was with me! Why on earth did he say he was with Angora?'

'He was with Angora,' said Lazlo in a level voice.

'For heaven's sake,' said Bella crossly, 'I know I was with him.'

'You weren't, you were with me.'

'Don't be ridiculous. I know it was pitch dark, but I couldn't mistake Steve. I recognized him by his aftershave, Black Opal.' Then she gave a gasp of horror.

'Oh no! It couldn't have been!'

'I'm afraid it was, darling,' said Lazlo. 'I was one of the stars of the Footlights when I was at Cambridge. It isn't very difficult to imitate Steve's American accent. I'm the same height and build as he is, our hair is more or less the same length. All I had to do was to douse myself in that rather noxious aftershave he uses – and, er, well, just leave the rest to nature.'

For a minute Bella was speechless, then she screamed, 'You bastard, you bastard! You tricked me into thinking Steve was still in love with me, and into breaking it off with Rupert, and what's more, I practically let you rape me.'

Lazlo laughed and helped himself to another drink. 'I must say I enjoyed that bit. I'd never have dreamt you could be so passionate. We must arrange an action replay sometime.'

Bella gave a snarl of rage like a maddened animal.

'Dirty, lousy son of a bitch,' she shouted. 'You've ruined my life.'

'What play did you say that in?' he said, still laughing.

His amusement snapped her last thread of control. Gibbering incoherently, she jumped to her feet and leapt at him trying to claw his face.

'Stop it,' he said, catching her wrists. 'Unless you want your eyes blacked. I don't have any scruples about hitting women.'

For a moment she glared at him, then, realizing herself beaten, she tore her hands away and slumped on the sofa.

The door bell rang. Bella ran out into the hall and opened the door. Two men with hard, inquisitive faces stood outside.

'Miss Parkinson,' said one of them. 'Congratulations on your release. Can we ask you a few questions?'

'No, you can't,' said Lazlo.

He pulled Bella back into the flat.

'Mr. Henriques, Mr. Lazlo Henriques, isn't it?' said the second man in an oily voice.

'Get out,' said Lazlo icily.

They wilted as he slammed the door in their faces.

'How did you know I didn't want to talk to them?' Bella said furiously.

'You haven't got time.' He glanced at his watch. 'You're due on stage in an hour's time.'

'Don't be stupid, they'll have got an understudy.'

'They haven't. I rang Roger and told him you'd been let out!'

'But I can't go on, not after what's happened.' She collapsed on to a chair. 'I'm exhausted and my hair's dirty.'

'Don't be so bloody wet,' Lazlo said brutally. 'Whatever your faults, I thought you'd got guts.'

There was a crowd of reporters waiting outside the theatre, but Lazlo just elbowed them out of the way. If Bella hadn't loathed him so much, she would have been speechless that anyone could swear as fluently as he could.

In her dressing room Rosie Hassell was waiting in a petticoat and a fever of excitement.

'Bella, darling, what drama! How on earth did you get off so quickly?'

'That snake pulled strings,' Bella said, pointing at Lazlo, who was just behind her.

Roger Field popped in just before the five minute call.

'Bella, darling,' he said. 'Thank God you made it. How do you feel?'

'Utterly hellish,' said Bella through chattering teeth. 'I've just been sick.'

'All that smoked salmon and brandy,' sighed Lazlo. 'What a tragedy.'

Bella ignored him. 'I may be sick again any minute,' she said to Roger.

'It'll be your entrails next,' said Lazlo. 'Have you got any whisky, Roger?'

Before the performance Roger went on stage and told the audience Bella had been released and cleared of all charges. When she made her first entrance there were a few isolated claps. Then a storm of applause followed and the audience cheered their heads off. Bella nearly broke down.

At the end of the play she received the biggest ovation of her career. But she felt like a husk, completely exhausted, very near to tears. In a dream she received congratulations from the rest of the cast, and had just finished changing when Lazlo walked into her dressing-room.

'Can't you knock?' she said crossly.

'Don't be silly,' he said, taking her arm. 'Come on, we can't fend off the Press any longer.'

'I'm going home by myself,' she said, snatching her arm

away, and, running down the stairs, she tugged open the stage door. Immediately, she was blinded by a volley of flash bulbs and the whirring of television cameras.

'There she is,' shouted a hundred voices.

'Oh, no,' she yelped in horror, and retreated, slamming the door.

In the end it was the same rat race as before, Lazlo protecting her with his arms and Roger Field fending off the crowd. Somehow Lazlo got her into his car, and again, almost before she could draw breath, they seemed to be out on the M4 steaming towards Oxford.

'Where are we off to now?' she asked listlessly.

'To stay with some friends of mine in the country.'

'I don't want to stay with any of your bloody friends, not if they're anything like you.'

'They're not,' said Lazlo calmly. 'She's a singer, he writes. You'll like them.'

'I haven't anything to wear.'

'You won't need anything. Cass'll lend you a bikini.'

He turned on the wireless and the hot summer night was suddenly flooded with Mozart. Bella listened to those lovely liquid notes pouring forth like a nightingale, and suddenly the terrible realization that Steve didn't love her any more swept over her. Unable to stop herself, she broke into a storm of weeping. Lazlo took absolutely no notice and let her cry.

Finally, when she reached the gulping stage, he said, 'There's a hipflask in the dashboard; help yourself.'

'No thank you.'

Heartless beast, she thought furiously. He tricked me, he pretended to be Steve. If Chrissie hadn't started screaming, he'd have certainly gone the whole hog and screwed me. A hot wave of shame swept over her at the thought of how much she'd enjoyed it at the time.

They had turned off the motorway into deep country now. Cow parsley brushed against the moving car, a huge moon was gliding in and out of transparent wisps of cloud. Finally, Lazlo drew up near a big rambling house, covered in wistaria. Almost at once a woman came running out.

'Darlings,' she shouted. 'You have made good time. How lovely to see you.'

'This is Bella,' said Lazlo. 'She's brought nothing with her, so you'll have to lend her everything. I'll just put the car away.'

The woman hugged Bella. 'My name's Cass,' she said. 'Lazlo tells me you've been having the most awful time. I do hate the Press when their blood's up.'

They went into a huge untidy room with crumbs all over the floor, bowls of drooping flowers and two grand pianos covered with books and music.

A man with spectacles on top of his head put down his book and came forward to welcome Bella.

'I escaped up to London for your first night. You were superb. Come and sit down and I'll get you a drink.'

Cass plonked herself on the sofa opposite Bella and stretched out fat legs, burnt red by the sun.

'Grenville's been in love with you for years, ever since he saw you on television once.'

Grenville blushed. 'I suppose we haven't got any ice, darling?'

'None at all,' said Cass cheerfully. 'The fridge is so frozen up I can't get the ice tray back in.'

When he had gone out she said, 'I didn't know the set-up, so I've put you and Lazlo in different rooms, but he's in a huge double bed so you can always join him.'

'Oh no!' said Bella, horrified into dropping her guard. 'I'd rather sleep with a cobra than Lazlo.'

'How are the children?' said Lazlo, walking into the room, his arms full of bottles of drink.

Bella went scarlet. How much had he heard of her last remark?

'The children are away this weekend, thank God,' said Cass. 'I do love them, but it's bliss when they're away. They're boys,' she added to Bella, 'ten, eight and seven.'

'I've brought them some gin,' said Lazlo. 'I know they like it.'

Cass laughed. 'What are you doing after *Othello*?' she said to Bella.

'*The Seagull* – we start rehearsing on Monday.'

For the first time in days she felt at home. So much so that half an hour later she wasn't too shy to ask if she might go up to bed.

CHAPTER FOURTEEN

She slept until lunchtime, then got up, bathed and washed her hair. To her annoyance the orange rinse still wouldn't come out and her hair had gone impossibly fluffy like candy floss. She found Lazlo in the garden, his feet up on a table, reading the racing news, drinking champagne and tearing a chicken apart. He was wearing only a pair of dirty white trousers, and his swarthy skin was already turning brown.

'Where are the others?' she said.

'Working. Have some chicken?'

'No thank you. I'm not hungry.' It was a lie. She was starving.

He poured her out a glass of champagne and said, 'I do hope you're not going to be boring and sulk the whole weekend. I'm about to ring my bookmaker. I fancy Bengal Freedom, Safety Pin and Happy Harry. Shall I put a fiver on each of them for you?'

Bella picked up the paper and scanned it.

'No,' she said coldly. 'I prefer Merry Peasant, Early Days, and Campbell's Pride in the four o'clock.'

'They haven't got a dog's chance,' said Lazlo. 'Still, if you want to waste your money.'

After he'd gone inside she skimmed the rest of the paper. On the front page was a picture of her and Lazlo leaving the theatre.

'Who stole the diamond?' screamed the banner headline. 'Henriques mystery thickens as Bella declared innocent.'

With a beating heart she read the rest of the story, but there was nothing mentioned about her past. Thank God her public image was still intact.

'I've backed your horses for you,' said Lazlo, returning with another bottle of champagne.

She put down the paper and pointedly picked up her book,

trying to concentrate. Lazlo looked at the jacket. 'It's junk,' he said. 'How far have you got?'

'Page two hundred and fifty,' snapped Bella.

'Oh, yes, that's the bit just before page two hundred and fifty-one,' said Lazlo.

Bella ignored him.

She later had the indignity of watching the three horses Lazlo had backed romping home several lengths clear in three successive races. Her horses weren't even placed.

'You owe me fifteen pounds,' said Lazlo. 'I shan't press you for payment.'

Not trusting herself to speak, Bella went off for a walk. Even the bosky greenness everywhere couldn't cure her bad temper. By the time she reached the village shop, however, hunger overcame her and she bought two huge cream buns. She was just wandering back to the house, stuffing her face with one of them, when a dark green Mercedes glided down the road towards her. Choking with rage she turned her bulging cheeks towards the hedgerow.

'So glad you've recovered your appetite,' said Lazlo in amusement.

Cass cooked a marvellous dinner and, afterwards, Bella offered to wash up. Lazlo said he'd help her. But at exactly ten o'clock, after he'd given her back a third plate to wash because it still had mustard on the bottom, something snapped inside her.

Picking up the remains of the duck, she hurled it at Lazlo, missing him of course. Then she selected a very ripe peach and chucked it against the wall, then she kicked over Cass's music stand.

Lazlo started to laugh, 'Tell me, Bella, what are you going to do when you grow up?'

'Stop sending me up,' she screamed. Then she started breaking plates. That had Lazlo worried.

'Pack it in,' he snapped. Then, when she wouldn't, he slapped her extremely hard across the face. For a minute she glared at him, her eyes watering from the pain. She gave a sob and fled upstairs. In her bedroom her rage evaporated. Feeling bitterly ashamed of herself, she undressed and got into bed.

She lay still, listening to approaching thunder – her eyelids feeling as though they'd been pinned back from her eyes. She heard Cass and Grenville come to bed, laughing fondly. At last she drifted into an uneasy sleep.

It was the most terrifying dream she'd ever had. She was suffocating, drowning, unable to escape. Then she started screaming. Suddenly the room was flooded with light – Lazlo was standing in the doorway. The next moment he'd crossed the room and taken her in his arms.

'It's all right, baby, it's all right. It's only a bad dream.'

She could feel the warmth from his body. His fingers beneath her shoulder blades. What did it matter now that he was the person she loathed most in the world? He was at least a human being.

'I can't take any more,' she sobbed. 'I get this nightmare over and over again. I dream I'm drowning in blood – and I know it's my mother's. Oh God,' she buried her face in her hands.

'Come on. Talk about it.'

'I can't,' she whispered. Then, suddenly, everything came pouring out. She wasn't really talking to Lazlo, but to herself.

'I've always lied about my past,' she said in a choked voice. 'I was so ashamed of it. My mother was very respectable, the daughter of a Christian Science minister. But she fell in love with my father. He was divine, but as bent as a corkscrew. My mother didn't realize he'd been in prison four times for larceny even before she married him. For a bit he tried to go straight, but he kept getting sacked from different jobs. Then I was born. There was no money, and my mother was forced to go out to work.'

'Go on,' said Lazlo.

'She worked as a char, in other people's houses, but money finally got so short my father stole the church funds. My mother found the money under the floorboards, and she went straight to the minister, her father, and told him. That night they confronted my father and said they were going to the police. Can you imagine it? Grassing on your own family? My father made a bolt for it There was a fight; my grandfather fell and hit his head on the fender, and later he died in hospital. My father got life imprisonment for murder. My mother never visited him. He died in prison ten years later, from T.B.'

She paused and the faded mirror at the end of the room glinted gold with a strange rose-yellow flash. A violent crack of thunder split the air. Rain exploded from the sky.

'It was during the court case that my mother discovered my father was already married and I was il-il . . .' she gagged over the word.

'Illegitimate,' said Lazlo.

Bella nodded. 'My mother never smiled again. She moved to another part of Yorkshire, a little town called Nalesworth where no one knew her. She went on working as a daily and saved enough money to send me to a good school. But I hated it. All the other girls laughed at my ugly clothes and my thick accent. My mother was continually terrified I was going to take after my father. I look like him, you see. She used to beat me and lock me for hours in a darkened room, while she sallied forth to church meetings.

'I grew to hate her.' Bella's voice was so quiet now against the hiss of the rain, that Lazlo could hardly hear it. 'I used to dream and dream of escaping to London and becoming an actress. When I was seventeen they discovered she had cancer. But being a Christian Scientist she wouldn't let them give her any drugs. She must have been in agony, and it made her far more vicious. She used to drag her body round the house, running her fingers along the furniture to see if I'd dusted properly. We hadn't any money so I had to leave school and take a job in the local draper's shop.

'And then I met Steve.' She paused. 'He was working at one of the local discos. He was the most beautiful man I'd ever seen. He seemed to exude Hollywood glamour, the bright lights and freedom. Needless to say, he seduced me the first time I went out with him. In the end my mother found out. She ranted and raved, but she was too weak to do anything about it.

'One morning I heard two girls gossiping in the shop about Steve, saying he was seducing half the West Riding and running up bills everywhere. I went mad. I rushed round to his digs and found he'd walked out without even saying goodbye to me. He'd left no address. I knew my mother was dying, but I spent all day and all night combing the town for him. I got home at four o'clock in the morning. Two neighbours were with my mother. She was in a coma. She never recovered.'

Bella was shaking like a leaf now, trying to stop herself from crying.

'They all hated me in the town,' she said. 'They drew their curtains and whispered behind their hands about how evil I was. For three days I was alone in the house, surrounded by all those damn wreaths of lilies. But I couldn't think about anything except Steve leaving me. I was half crazy with misery. It was only after a while that I realized what I'd done to my mother. Then the nightmares started.'

'What happened then?'

'I came South. There was a little money left when the house was sold. I got a scholarship to RADA, changed my name to Bella Parkinson, told everyone my father was a librarian, my mother a schoolmistress. Lies I told so often I almost came to believe them.'

She looked down at her hands, 'Now you know everything.'

'I knew most of it already.'

'You did? But how? Did Steve tell you?'

'A little. I've got a good information service.'

Bella gave a hollow laugh. 'No wonder you didn't want me to marry Rupert. The bastard daughter of a murderer. Hardly Debrett is it?'

'I didn't care a damn about your background.'

She looked up in surprise. Lazlo didn't seem appalled, or angry or contemptuous, or any of the other things she'd expected anyone she'd ever told the truth to be. For once his dark mocking face looked completely serious.

'Look,' he said. 'It doesn't matter what happened before in your life. No one minds except you. It's what you are – talented, funny.' He glanced down at her blotched, tear-stained face and smiled slightly. 'Yes, even beautiful, that's important. The Henriques have a pretty seamy past if you study it. Only four centuries back they were raping, looting and murdering to get the things they wanted. They just did it a few hundred years earlier than your father did. Besides, he wasn't a murderer. He just killed someone in a fight.'

'Like you did,' said Bella.

'Like I killed Miguel Rodriguez,' said Lazlo, his face hardening.

Gently, he laid her back in bed, and got to his feet. 'I'm going to get you a sleeping pill.'

It was only when he came back that she realized he was still dressed in the black shirt and dirty white trousers he'd been wearing all evening.

'Why weren't you in bed?' she said.

'I was reading. I don't sleep a great deal. There's usually something, or – er – someone better to do.'

She suddenly realized she was only wearing a very transparent nightgown, and that Lazlo had been holding her in his arms, and that only two nights ago, when he'd pretended to be Steve, he'd practically raped her. She felt herself going scarlet and slunk down under the sheets.

'I'm sorry,' she muttered. 'I shouldn't have bored you with my problems.'

'Bella,' he said in amazement, 'you're apologizing to me. Are you sure you're feeling all right?'

'Don't tease me,' she said in a strangled voice. 'I'm not in the mood.'

He laughed. 'Hell being a woman isn't it? It's just not your century.'

CHAPTER FIFTEEN

SHE felt like a convalescent recovering from a very bad attack of flu the next day. She found herself impossibly shy of Lazlo, hardly able to meet his eyes. Most of the day she slept in the sun. And in the evening she sobbed herself stupid over *The King And I* on television. She also felt quite unnecessarily irritated when Angora telephoned Lazlo from France where she was filming, and he took the telephone into the other room.

Next day he'd driven Bella back to London to start rehearsals on *The Seagull*, and now here she was, three days later, sulking in the hairdresser's because he hadn't even rung her up to see how she was.

Bernard, her hairdresser, picked up a strand of her hair.

'That's a bit of a mistake, duckie,' he said. The pink rinse had turned green in the sun.

'I'll say,' said Bella crossly. 'I've decided to go back to my natural colour.' Bernard looked appalled, 'But what on earth is it?'

'A sort of dark mouse, not unattractive.'

'But, darling, you're crazy. You've been blonde for years, no one'll recognize you. It'll ruin your image.'

'I've got to play a very mousey girl in my next play.'

Alas, no woman is a dedicated artist to her hairdresser.

Bernard grinned slyly. 'Don't give me that, dearie. You've met some nice, straight bloke who you think doesn't like dyed hair.'

'Nonsense,' said Bella crossly. But she blushed crimson.

The weather grew even hotter. She had to rehearse all afternoon. It was impossibly stuffy in the theatre. She was just getting her teeth into her part when something happened to wreck her concentration. Five minutes later she was back in her dressing-room.

'What on earth's the matter?' said Rosie Hassell in alarm. 'It was going so well.'

'It's Johnnie,' stormed Bella, glaring at the handsome blond boy who played Konstantin, who was leaning against her dressing-table.

'Didn't you see him sneaking on to the stage and letting loose that toad. He knows I'm terrified of toads.'

Johnnie started to laugh. 'Bella, angel, the scene is played beside a lake. It should be absolutely crawling with frogs and toads and things. I was only trying to inject a little realism into the act.'

'You were not,' shouted Bella. 'You were trying to put the fear of God into me.'

'Oh well.' Johnnie shrugged his shoulders. 'If you're going to be stuffy.'

'I am. I bloody am.'

Roger Field stood in the doorway frowning. Two of his leading players hurling abuse at each other cannot have been the most edifying sight, but Bella was past caring.

'I'll report you to Equity and get you kicked out,' she screamed at Johnnie.

'That's enough, Bella,' said Roger. 'The whole theatre can hear you.'

'I don't care,' Bella shouted. 'Do you know what he did? He put this toad . . .'

'All right, pack it in, Johnnie. Take that toad back to the Thames, or wherever you found it. I'll talk to you later.'

Grinning broadly, Johnnie slouched out of the room.

'I'll kill you, kill you, kill you!' Bella screamed after him.

'Stop bawling like a fishwife,' said Roger. 'There's someone to see you.'

'I don't want to see anyone,' snapped Bella. 'I want you to stop that horrible boy putting toads in my . . .' Her voice trailed off, for in the doorway stood Lazlo.

'I'll leave her to you,' said Roger. 'I hope you make a better job of calming her down than I did.'

Bella was speechless for a minute. Then she said, 'What are you doing here?'

'Watching your rehearsal,' said Lazlo. 'I was going to tell you how good you were, but I'm not sure if you deserve it. I'm glad you get abusive with other people besides me,' he said.

'It's not funny.' Bella slumped down in her chair and gazed at herself in the mirror. Mousey hair scraped back in an elastic band, shiny face without a scrap of make-up, shirt soaking with sweat, splitting jeans. Oh, damn, damn, damn. She'd meant to be so silken and beautiful next time she met him.

'What do you want?' she said, ungraciously.

'I was going to ask you out to dinner, but I won't if you're going to be so ratty.'

'Oh, well,' she blushed and shuffled her feet.

'I've got two Arabs to entertain, I'm meeting them at eight. Can you be ready in a quarter of an hour?'

'But I haven't got anything to wear,' Bella wailed.

Lazlo got to his feet. 'You'd better borrow something,' he said. 'I'm going to talk business with Roger. By the way,' he added, as he went out of the door, 'I like the hair. It's a distinct improvement.'

The Arabs were jolly and fat, and ate all Bella's potatoes and steak at dinner. She had borrowed a pair of shorts and an orange T-shirt from Rosie, which was much too tight across the bust.

Her suntan was beginning to fade. She kept wishing she could think of witty things to say.

The Arabs wanted to make a night of it and kept muttering about strip clubs, but Lazlo managed to extricate himself and Bella about midnight. They didn't speak as he drove across London. They stopped at a traffic light. Please make it stay red for ever, she prayed. She held her breath when they came to Hyde Park, but he turned left. She was appalled by the joy that flooded over her as she realized he was taking her back to his flat instead of hers.

As Lazlo poured out drinks for them both, she studied him carefully, examining the thick, black hair curling over his collar, the broad shoulders in the immaculate white suit, the sunburnt hands shooting soda into the glasses, and suddenly she felt quite giddy with lust.

What's happening to me? she thought in horror. Five days ago I was madly in love with Steve, and now all I can do is long and long and long to be in bed with Lazlo.

As he handed her a drink, their hands touched. Jumping as though he'd burnt her, she seized the glass and bolted over to the window. It's all right for him, she thought in panic. Riverboat gambler, with the morals of an alley cat, and a million light years of sexual experience under his belt. All he has to do is throw a little soft soap around and he'll have me eating out of his hand.

Lazlo took off his jacket and hung it on the back of a chair.

'You're very quiet,' he said. 'What's eating you?'

Bella took a deep breath. 'I know you're only being nice to me,' she blurted out, 'because you want me to fall for you. Just to make sure I won't go back to Rupert.'

Lazlo sighed. 'That's a very silly, childish remark. I did hope you'd given up making remarks like that.'

Bella looked mutinous. There was a pause.

Then she stammered. 'All right, I'm sorry. I was being ungracious.'

He smiled. 'Good girl to apologize. Come over here.'

'No,' said Bella in a strangled voice. 'I can't do it, I can't be another of your one-night-stands, just to amuse you for tonight because you can't sleep.'

'My dear child, what are you on about?'

The telephone rang. Lazlo took no notice.

'Hadn't you better answer it?' Bella said shakily.

'All right.' He picked up the receiver, not taking his eyes off her face.

'Hullo? Yes, Aunt Constance, *what* an unexpected pleasure.' He grinned at Bella and raised his eyes to heaven.

Suddenly the smile was wiped off his face.

'What's that?' he snarled. 'When did this happen? Why wasn't I told before? Have you told the police? All right, I'll come straight over.'

The scar down the side of his face was like a livid gash as he put down the receiver. His eyes were blazing with rage.

'What's the matter?' said Bella.

'Chrissie. She's been kidnapped. They want two million pounds ransom.'

CHAPTER SIXTEEN

LAZLO stormed the great dark green Mercedes through the deserted London streets, shooting traffic lights, squealing the wheels round corners. Bella sat frozen with horror beside him.

'But how on earth did it happen?' she whispered.

'Chrissie went out to post a letter at half past six and didn't come back,' said Lazlo. 'Aunt Constance and Uncle Charles were out, and the first anyone realized she'd disappeared was when Steve turned up at nine to take her to some party, and she wasn't there.'

'Steve was taking her out?' Bella said sharply.

Lazlo shot her a sidelong glance. 'Now Angora's gone to France,' he said, 'Steve seems to have transferred his rather liberal affections to Chrissie.'

Bella flushed. 'What happened then?'

'The kidnappers telephoned at eleven-thirty, saying they'd got Chrissie and they'd release her unhurt as long as we paid up two million pounds and didn't call the police.'

Outwardly he was perfectly calm now. The harsh, swarthy face betrayed no emotion. But a muscle quivered in his cheek and his hand shook badly as he lit a cigarette.

If only I were Angora, thought Bella miserably, I'd fling my arms round him and find all the right things to say to comfort him.

She was further thrown by the fact that when they reached the Henriques' house the door was answered by Rupert. He had obviously just got off the plane from Zurich. His luggage littered the hall.

'Thank God you've arrived,' he said to Lazlo. 'Poor darling little Chrissie. What the hell are we going to do about her? Everyone's being absolutely useless. My mother's having hysterics at the thought of parting with two million pounds. My father's shipped enough liquor to float the *QE2* and that snake Steve is ...' Suddenly he seemed to notice Bella and pulled himself together. 'Oh, hullo,' he said perfunctorily.

In the drawing-room they found Charles standing in front of the fire, with glazed eyes, and Steve on the sofa, drinking brandy, and managing to look completely at home and the picture of concern at the same time. Constance, massive in maroon satin, strode down the room towards them.

'Where on earth have you been, Lazlo? Out on the tiles as usual, I suppose,' she added sourly. Then she glared at Bella. 'And what's she doing here? You must talk some sense into Rupert and Charles. They won't call the police.'

'Quite right,' said Lazlo. 'The fewer people who know about this, the better.' He turned to Charles. 'We'd better work out the fastest way to get the cash together.'

Constance looked appalled. 'But we can't raise that amount. We shall be ruined. I have enough trouble making ends meet as it is. Why don't you let the police sort it out?'

'If you call the police,' said Lazlo brutally, 'you'll only panic the kidnappers into bumping Chrissie off.'

'Don't use those awful words,' said Constance. 'That child was like a daughter to me.'

'Oh, Gawd,' said Rupert rudely. 'Don't be such a hypocrite. You treated Chrissie like a slave. She never stopped running errands for you.'

Constance compressed her lips. 'It was Chrissie's fault in a way,' she said to Steve. 'I always told her if she went out without a hat she'd get picked up by undesirable types.'

'Those men were lying in wait for her,' said Rupert through clenched teeth. 'Don't be so bloody stupid.'

Constance turned purple. 'How dare you speak to me like that?' she said. 'I've had enough to cope with. All the strain of Gay's wedding, and then you getting engaged to that terrible ...' Then she remembered that Bella was in the room, and just stopped herself in time. But before anyone could feel embarrassed, she launched into a further hysterical tirade against Rupert.

Lazlo looked at her reflectively, and then said, in a surprisingly gentle voice, 'This must be a terrible strain for you, Aunt Constance. You must be exhausted. I don't expect you've had any dinner either. Why don't you go to bed, and we'll get someone to bring you something on a tray.'

'How could you expect me to eat at a time like this?' said Constance, but she looked mollified. 'Perhaps I should keep my strength up. I suppose I could just manage a chicken sandwich.'

Steve got to his feet and gave Constance one of his devastating smiles. 'I'll go and have a word in the kitchen,' he said.

'You're such a comfort to me, Steve,' Constance could be heard saying as she went up the stairs.

Lazlo, Rupert and Charles immediately settled down to discuss raising the money, but Charles was obviously having difficulty concentrating.

'I think I'll hit the hay, too,' he said, tottering towards the door. 'Thank you for coping so admirably with Constance, Lazlo.'

As Charles left the room, Steve came back.

'Half a capon and a vat of french fries are on their way upstairs to Constance. That should keep her quiet,' he said to Lazlo. 'I can't tell you how appalled I am about Chrissie. I've only known her a fortnight, but it's long enough to realize what a great kid she is.'

'You didn't realize anything of the kind,' snapped Rupert. 'You were just after her bread.'

'Shut up, Rupe,' said Lazlo, and went back to talking about money.

Bella studied Steve surreptitiously, and wondered how she could ever have loved him to such distraction. Everything about him revolted her now. He's just a handsome hunk of nothing, she thought. Then she turned to Rupert, sitting in the window seat, with his head in his hands, completely gone to pieces. Then she looked at Lazlo. That muscle was still pounding in his cheek, and she suddenly realized the titanic dependability and strength of the man – and how much it must be costing him in sheer teeth-gritting self-control not to give way to sniping and panic like the others.

As unexpected as an extra step at the bottom of a flight of stairs, it came upon her. It was Lazlo she was in love with.

At that moment he looked at her. 'You're tired?' he said.

'I ought to go,' she muttered, terrified that he might read what was in her mind.

'I'll drive you home,' said Steve.

'Rupert'll take her,' said Lazlo. 'I want to pick your brains about raising cash in Buenos Aires, Steve.'

Bella didn't speak on the way home, desperately trying to control the raging emotions inside her. But when they reached the flat, she asked Rupert if he wanted to come up for a drink.

He shook his head. 'I must get back. Oh, hell, Bella, what am I going to do? I took Chrissie so much for granted, treating her like a tiresome kid-sister, and now, suddenly, she's gone . . .'

'You realize you're in love with her.'

He looked up, his face haggard. 'Yes, I am. I thought I was going to shoot myself last week because you wouldn't marry me, but now Chrissie's in such terrible danger, I know it's her I love, and I don't suppose I'll ever see her again.'

Bella put her arms round him. 'There, there, it's going to be all right. Lazlo'll find her for you.'

'Oh, he'll get her back if anyone can,' said Rupert. 'With all his mates in the underworld, he can pull strings like nobody's business, but I've got a horrible feeling this isn't a straightforward money kidnapping, that it's all got something to do with Miguel Rodriguez.'

Bella's heart missed a beat. 'The man Lazlo killed?'

Rupert nodded. 'Miguel's brother, Juan, has been trying to pay Lazlo back ever since.'

'What was the real story behind it?'

'Miguel and Juan Rodriguez ran a vice ring in South America. They had Buenos Aires so completely sewn up. The police were terrified of them. Miguel had a much younger wife called Maria, whom he treated like dirt. She and Lazlo fell in love and had a raging affair. Miguel found out and pulled a knife on Lazlo in a bar. There was a fight. Miguel was killed.

'The next day – although no one could pin it on him – Juan had acid thrown in Maria's face. Her beauty was ruined. She couldn't bear Lazlo to see her like that. A few days later she committed suicide. The police were too scared of Juan to do anything about it, but Lazlo and he have been stalking each other like a pair of tigers ever since. I think it's Juan's boys who have nicked Chrissie, and if they have, they'll never let her go alive, however much we fork out. That's what's crucifying Lazlo.'

'Was she very beautiful, Miguel's wife?' said Bella, trying to sound casual.

'Maria? Oh, absolutely ravishing. I don't think Lazlo's ever really got over her committing suicide.'

After she'd let herself into her flat, Bella sat for hours, lacerated with jealousy at the thought of Maria Rodriguez.

CHAPTER SEVENTEEN

Two days dragged by with no news of Chrissie. Bella tried to throw herself into rehearsals, but she could think of nothing but Lazlo and the hell he must be going through. She also tried not to feel disappointed when he didn't telephone her. He must have far too much on his mind.

On the evening of the third day she came out of the theatre absolutely dead beat. She had rehearsed all day, followed by a gruelling performance of *Othello* in the evening. The audience had been as unreceptive as blotting paper, particularly a coach load from the Mothers' Union in the stalls who had talked and laughed through the last act.

It was a dark, hot, sultry night, with no stars and a suggestion of thunder. She was wearing only a skimpy red and white spotted dress. The smell of frying garlic and onions from a nearby Italian Restaurant made her feel slightly sick. She decided to walk part of the way home. She passed a telephone box and resisted the temptation to go inside and ring Lazlo to find out if he had any news of Chrissie. She would be too tongue-tied to do it properly.

You *must* stop thinking about him, she told herself angrily.

She turned right into a road only dimly lit by a few street lamps. Suddenly, she saw a cigarette glow in the dark and a figure stepped towards her.

She jumped nervously as a voice whispered, 'Bella.'

Then she saw a gleam of silver blond hair, and her nervousness turned to irritation. It was Steve.

'What the hell are you doing here?' she snapped.

'I *must* talk to you.'

'Well I don't want to talk to you. I've got nothing to say to you – nothing.'

'Honey,' he said urgently. 'For Pete's sake listen, I'm on the level. I've found out where Chrissie is.'

Bella turned towards him with a gasp.

'Are you sure? Is she O.K.?'

'I don't know. They're holding her in some deserted warehouse in the East End. It sounds like a pretty amateur job to me. One of the gang got cold feet and grassed to a mate of mine.'

'Have you told Lazlo?'

'I can't get hold of him. He went to the races this afternoon and hasn't been seen since.'

'Well, what are we waiting for?' said Bella, not stopping to think.

'I'm parked over there,' said Steve, pointing to a car under the trees.

Bella ran towards it.

'Come on. We mustn't waste any time.'

Her only thought was how pleased Lazlo would be if they found Chrissie.

Steve opened the front door for her, and she was just bending forward to get in when a voice in the back said, in a thick foreign accent, 'Don't try anything silly. We've got you covered.'

And she saw the gleam of a pistol butt.

Giving a scream, she backed out again, against Steve, but he shoved her violently into the car. The next moment something hard and metallic hit her on the head. And simultaneously it seemed, someone reached in front of her, suffocating her with a sweet-smelling cloth. She had the feeling she was falling forward, crashing her head on the dashboard of the car as she went. Next moment all was blackness.

She had no idea how long she was unconscious. When she came to, there was an excruciating pain pounding through her head, and she realized she was in a moving car. There was thick cloth tied over her eyes, ropes were biting into her wrists and ankles, and she could feel the back of her head bleeding still, the blood dripping onto the back of her neck.

She groaned and retched.

'Steve, I'm going to be sick.'

No one said anything, but the car slowed down. She was lifted out like a sack of potatoes and someone held her head while she retched and retched, sobbing with pain, humiliation and terror.

'Let me go, please let me go. I'm innocent. I haven't done anything.'

Next moment someone was forcing her mouth open. She struggled frenziedly as they poured liquid down her throat. They were trying to poison her. Then she realized it was only brandy. Her throat was burning. She thought she was going to throw up again.

They gave her another slug. She began to feel a bit better.

Hastily she was bundled back in the car. Still no one spoke to her, and they set off again. Lulled by the brandy, she decided not to ask any questions. Why provoke them?

They must have driven about four hours after that. She kept worrying about the matinée next day, and how there was no way she was going to make it. And how the understudy would probably be much better than her. Then she thought of Lazlo and what he would think if he knew she'd been kidnapped – probably wouldn't care anyway.

But why should they snatch her? Perhaps if they still thought Rupert was crazy about her, she might pull in a bigger ransom. But Steve had been there the other night. It must have been quite obvious that Rupert was only crazy about Chrissie now, and wasn't in love with her any more.

Her mind reeled in turmoil. She'd never trusted Steve, but in all her dealings with him, she'd never dreamed he was a gangster, perhaps tied up with a cold-blooded murderer like Juan Rodriguez. If it hadn't been for her, he would never have been able to meet the Henriques family and ingratiate himself into their good books and make off with Chrissie so easily. She was sure now he was behind Chrissie's kidnapping as well.

Then, with a shiver, she remembered Rupert saying that if Juan's boys nicked Chrissie, they'd never let her out alive. Perhaps she'd get acid thrown in her face like Maria Rodriguez.

The anaesthetizing effect of the brandy was wearing off. The pain in her head was excruciating. Panic took over. 'Oh, Lazlo, help me, help me,' she whimpered.

Someone kicked her viciously in the ankle.

'Shut your bloody mouth,' said the same thick foreign accent, rough with fear and anxiety.

She could feel the tension in the car. Someone was beside

her in the back, perhaps two in the front. She could tell they were really scared. There was a sickly sweet goat smell of sweat, and over and over again she heard matches flare as cigarettes were chain-smoked. Being blindfold, her whole nervous system picked up things quicker.

She had realized it must be nearly morning when someone turned on the wireless. It was the six o'clock news. She waited breathlessly.

Mrs. Thatcher had taken Mr. Wilson to task during a late night sitting in the House. Australia had devalued the dollar. A leopard had escaped from the Zoo. A Royal Princess had announced her engagement. The weather would be hot and sunny, although thundery showers were expected towards evening.

Bella slumped back in her seat in despair. No one would ever find her.

They were driving fast now, presumably to reach their destination before too many people were about, storming along straight roads, squealing round corners. It was getting hotter. She was desperate to go to the loo.

Finally, the car stopped, and they took her out. She felt a warm breeze on her arms and legs, and a distant smell of salt and the sound of the waves pounding.

Suddenly she was panicking that they were high up, near the sea, and they were going to push her over a cliff.

She was shaking uncontrollably. She started to cry again. Quickly someone put a hand over her mouth.

'Keep quiet,' snarled a voice, and she felt something cold and metallic jabbed in her back.

Then they sat down on the grass and took the ropes off her ankles, so she could walk. They must have moved her then a couple of miles. She felt people round her all the time, moving, walking and whispering. She could hear cows mooing, birds singing, and the hum of cars in the distance.

Now her feet were on gravel, crunching up a path. She could feel the relief of those around her, a lightening of tension.

She was stumbling over the threshold, a door slammed, a lock clicked. There was a smell of musty, unwashed house that took her straight back to her childhood in the slums. She felt the sweat pouring off her. Next moment someone ran downstairs and, taking her arm, dragged her upstairs and pushed her into a room.

Someone undid her hands. She felt her blindfold; it seemed to be held down with masking tape. The next moment someone had ripped it off, catching some of her hair. Her head was so tender, she screamed.

'Don't hurt her,' said the voice with the thick foreign accent.

She blinked in the half light. Two men stood in front of her. Both were masked. But she realized neither was Steve. One was very stocky with black hair, a black beard sticking out from under his mask, and massive shoulders.

The other was taller and slimmer, with thinning dark hair.

'Listen, baby,' he said. He also had a Spanish accent, but less strong than the other one. 'You're going to be here a long time. Don't do anything silly. If you want anything, we'll try and get it for you.'

'I must go to the loo,' said Bella desperately.

The taller one laughed. 'There's a bucket in the corner.'

She was flaming well going to wait till they'd gone.

'Where's Steve?' she said. 'Is he here?'

The taller one shook his head and showed her his gun.

'I repeat, don't try anything silly like escaping. There are five of us here guarding you.'

Suddenly Bella was terrified they'd taken off her blindfold, because she knew if one of them forgot their masks or if it slipped off they'd have to kill her.

They left her after that, and she had time to examine the room. It was very small, about ten feet by ten feet, and lit by a twenty watt bulb. A heavy wooden shutter was nailed over the window, the wallpaper was stained dirty brown, and thick dusty cobwebs hung from the smoke-grimed ceiling. The only furniture was a broken chair and the bucket in the corner.

She tried the bars on the window, but they were firmly nailed down. There were no weaknesses in the walls. Anyway, she'd bitten her nails so far down in the last few days they'd be no good for burrowing a hole.

A few minutes later another man came into the room to clean up the wound on the back of her head. He had long, blondish hair, was very thin, and had a quiet, soft voice with the same accent as the other two.

She found herself ridiculously grateful for the gentle way he handled her, warning her that the antiseptic was going to sting. She sensed he felt sorry for her. She noticed that he wore trousers that were too short, rather flashy yellow socks on his thin ankles and ill-fitting basket-weave shoes.

Afterwards she lay down and tried to make herself as comfortable as possible. Outside, she could hear them speaking to one another in Spanish. They *must* be Juan's boys.

Sometime in the afternoon the thin blond boy brought her in a cup of tea and baked beans on a piece of bread on a greasy tin plate. Starving, she wolfed the lot, then, two minutes later, threw it all up, only just reaching the bucket in time.

Her head seemed to be splitting open. Clutching it, she crouched on the floor, sobbing. She must get out, she was going mad. Then she remembered reading somewhere that if you could survive the first forty-eight hours of a kidnapping, you could survive anything. She must get a grip on herself.

Our Father which art in Heaven, she began.

She noticed they hadn't risked giving her a knife and fork with her food. She examined her face in the spoon. Her eyes were huge, her face pale and streaked with blood.

She decided to try and recite the whole of *Othello* – anything to keep her sane; but as she got to the third act, as Othello's jealousy is slowly awakened by Iago, her mind kept straying to Lazlo, reliving the moments they'd spent together, the fights they'd had, the weekend in the country when he'd held her in his arms after the nightmare. What was it he'd said? That she was funny, talented and beautiful.

She looked at her reflection in the spoon again. He wouldn't think she was beautiful now. She felt a black churning hatred against Steve.

At last, out of sheer exhaustion, she fell into an uneasy sleep.

CHAPTER EIGHTEEN

SHE was woken by crunching on the gravel outside. Light was no longer filtering through a crack in the shutters. She heard three knocks, then the front door being opened quickly and quietly, and then shut again, then whispered voices and a slight laugh and someone coming up the stairs past her door.

She still felt sick, but the pain in her head was receding a bit. She struggled to her feet, feeling stiff and dizzy. Her mouth tasted awful. She could feel a film of dirt when she ran her tongue over her teeth.

No Colgate ring of confidence for you, she thought, licking her fingers and trying to rub away the bloodstains on her cheeks.

Logic told her that if the kidnappers liked her and thought she was pretty they would be less likely to do her in.

She wondered who the latest arrival was, but she didn't have long to wait. Next minute the door opened and two men in masks came in, carrying guns. One was the stocky, bearded one; the other, whom she hadn't seen before, was taller, wearing very tight trousers over slightly overweight hips, and a dark blue shirt. He had a very large torso. She could see patches of hairy chest between each button.

'Come on, beauty,' he said, tying her hands up, in an oily, lisping voice that made Bella shiver. 'It's time for a little chat.'

They led her down the passage to a brightly lit room. In it were several chairs and a table covered with bottles, glasses and tins of food.

A man lounged on an old sofa. He was also masked, but Bella noticed he was wearing an expensive, if slightly too flashy, blue suit, expensive gold cuff-links and watch, a pale blue silk shirt and he smelt strongly of aftershave.

'Hi, Bella baby,' he said. 'What'll you drink?'

He had a nice voice, deep, slow and soft, with slight American overtones.

'We'll have her hands untied, too, Carlos,' he said to the stocky, bearded gunman.

'We don't want you to be any more uncomfortable than you need, and I guess we can trust you not to do anything silly.'

Why do they keep saying that, thought Bella, irrationally. Lazlo would say she was always doing silly things.

Carlos undid the rope with a bread knife. It had left purple marks on her wrists. The man on the sofa got up and rubbed them gently.

'You really shouldn't have tied them so tight,' he said reproachfully.

Bella was frightened by this soft approach. She could feel the sweat running down her sides.

'You'd like a drink,' he said. 'Scotch?'

Bella nodded.

'I'm afraid we don't run to ice.'

He poured her a large whisky and put the glass on a chair beside her.

She glanced round. The two guards leant against the door behind her, fingering their guns.

She picked up her glass, but her hand was shaking so much she could hardly get it to her mouth.

'You're frightened,' said the man in the blue suit. 'What are you afraid of?'

'Your mob haven't behaved with much gentleness so far.'

'You're afraid we might spoil your beauty. Forget it.'

He picked up the bread knife and started to cut the end off a cigar.

She noticed he had beautifully manicured hands, the nails slightly too long.

'Why have you brought me here?' she blurted out. 'It's tied up with Chrissie, isn't it?'

'Sure it is.'

'Is she O.K.?'

'She's just fine. Not bearing up under the strain as well as she might, but she's been cooped up longer than you have, and I guess she's led a much more cushy life than you – not used to roughing it. Not a great fan of yours, is she?'

Bella flushed. 'It's no business of yours.'

'Can't say I blame her. You took her boyfriend off her, didn't you?'

'I didn't,' said Bella, nettled, taking another slug of whisky. 'He came of his own accord.'

'I don't blame him,' he said, getting up from his chair, and running his hand down her face. 'You're very lovely,' he added softly as Bella flinched away. 'And I'm not surprised El Gatto's got the hots for you as well. He's been trying to cut Rupert out, hasn't he?'

Bella looked bewildered, then suddenly realized they meant Lazlo. 'No,' she said in a strangled voice. 'It's not true.'

Her early warning system wasn't working very well, but it seemed vital to convince him there was nothing between her and Lazlo – or she'd never get out alive.

'Is he going to be able to raise the dough?'

'Of course he will, but it takes time in the present economic climate.'

'Sure,' said the man in the blue suit.

'But he's got steel nerves, Lazlo,' Bella went on. 'He won't hand over a penny till he has assurances Chrissie's safe, and going to be handed back.'

'Well, to help him get his finger out, we'd like you to make a little tape tomorrow, telling him how much you're missing him and how miserable you are.'

Bella went white.

'No,' she said in a strangled voice. 'I couldn't do that.'

'I would if I were you. You'll find us very easy going as long as you agree to play ball.'

'Can I see Chrissie? Is she here too?'

'Sure, why not. She's in here.' He opened a door on the right and filled up her glass. 'Take your drink with you.'

Bella's first thought was how beautiful Chrissie had grown. She must have lost pounds. The black dress she'd been kidnapped in hung off her, her dark hair looked even darker because it was greasy, and her eyes were huge in her dead white face.

When she saw Bella she shrunk away.

'Go away!' she screamed. 'I don't want her near me. I hate her, I hate her!'

She collapsed on to the bed, sobbing hysterically.

The door closed behind Bella; a key clicked in the lock. She bent over Chrissie, close to tears herself.

'Please don't cry. It's going to be all right. Lazlo's going to raise the cash.'

'He's not! He's not! Why hasn't he raised it before then? Everyone's deserted me, and now they bring you in here to torture me.'

Bella knelt down beside her.

'Here, have some whisky.'

'I don't want any of their horrible booze,' said Chrissie, clenching her fists in a sudden spasm of misery. 'I haven't eaten anything since I've been here. Trust you to suck up to them and accept their beastly drink.'

And, swinging round towards Bella, she knocked the glass out of her hand so whisky spilled all over the floor and Bella's dress.

'I *hate* you! *hate* you!' she sobbed. 'Steve was your crooked friend. If you hadn't introduced him to us, this never would have happened. I wouldn't put it past you to be in this together.'

'I'm not anything to do with it,' said Bella, trying to be patient. 'I was as appalled as you to find that Steve was mixed up in it.'

'Then why have they grabbed you as well?' said Chrissie. 'I suppose they think Rupert would be more likely to persuade Lazlo to fork out two million pounds for you than he would be for me.' And she started to sob again.

'Look, please listen,' Bella said. 'It's all over between Rupert and me.'

Chrissie looked at her sullenly.

'You may have broken it off because you got bored with him, but he's still nuts about you.'

'He's not, I promise. He flew back from Zurich the night you were kidnapped. I've never seen anyone in such a state. Lazlo and I went round to Chichester Terrace the moment we heard the news. Lazlo started planning how to raise the cash. Constance was being her usual unspeakable self and Charles was too tight to be any use. But Rupert had gone completely to pieces. He absolutely tore a strip off Constance when she grumbled about raising so much money.'

'I don't believe you,' said Chrissie dully.

'Afterwards Rupert drove me home – only because Lazlo told him to,' she added hastily. 'He said he'd always taken you for granted because you'd always been there, a kind of kid sister ready to adore him. But now you were in danger, he realized it was you he loved all the time. He was absolutely demented with worry.'

'You're just saying it.'

'I'm not, I promise.'

Chrissie started to cry. Then like a child with a bedtime story, she said, 'Could you possibly tell me what you've just told me – all over again!'

Later Bella said, 'How the hell are we going to get out of here?'

'I don't think we can,' said Chrissie. 'They're all armed to the teeth. They scare the life out of me.'

'There was a blond one who was kind to me when he cleaned up the wound on my head,' said Bella.

'That's Diego,' said Chrissie. 'He's all right, but there's a spooky one called Pablo who hasn't said a word the whole time. He's got a finger missing on his right hand. And the really horrible one is Ricardo. He's the one who's bursting out of his shirts. Whenever he ties me up at night, he touches me far more than necessary. I'm sure he's going to try something soon – they all seem so jumpy and frustrated. I say, do you really think Rupert loves me?'

CHAPTER NINETEEN

THREE days passed with unbearable slowness. They listened to every news bulletin, but there was no mention of the kidnapping. Even Bella began to feel everyone had abandoned them. One of her greatest worries was stopping Chrissie from cracking up under the strain. But, in fact, it gave her something to do, fussing over the younger girl, seeing she ate something, keeping her cheerful. They talked incessantly, Chrissie babbling on about her childhood in South America, and about Rupert, and inevitably about Lazlo, Bella trying desperately not to appear too interested whenever his name was mentioned.

Now that Chrissie had lost so much weight, and her face had thinned down, she reminded Bella of him so poignantly. They had the same cheekbones, the same impassivity, the same smile that would light up a blacked-out city when suddenly they were amused.

On the second morning, the gunmen took Bella into the living-room and made her record a ridiculous tape to be sent to Lazlo and the family, begging them to raise the money as soon as possible, and not to contact the police. She had to read it over and over again, until they were satisfied with the stress and the timing.

'And at the end, say "I love you",' said Ricardo.

'I won't,' said Bella.

Ricardo held the gun to her temple, 'I would if I were you.'

'I love you very much,' whispered Bella.

'That should get El Gatto to pull his finger out,' said Ricardo.

Chrissie, who'd just been brought in to make her tape, overheard Bella's last remark.

'What the hell's going on?' she hissed to Bella as soon as they were locked up together again. 'You've been pulling a fast one all the time. Why did you say you loved Rupert just now. You are still after him.'

Bella found herself blushing. 'I'm not. The gunmen have got completely the wrong end of the stick. For some reason they're convinced Lazlo and I are mad about each other.'

Chrissie's mouth opened and shut, and then she started to laugh incredulously. 'You and Lazlo! God, they must be thick. If they only knew how much you loathe each other.'

Bella didn't wince. She was making great strides in self-control, but she found it very difficult not to react during the next day when Chrissie kept saying, 'You and Lazlo,' and going off into fits of laughter.

Chrissie, now she had Bella to protect her, slept a great deal. She had so many shocks in the last week to recover from. This left Bella plenty of time to observe her captors.

The smooth man in the light blue suit had left. He was probably, Bella decided, some henchman, fairly high up in the Rodriquez empire. Five others remained: Ricardo, the thug with the bulging muscles and the soft oily voice, Diego, the tall blond one with the gentle hands and voice, Carlos, stocky and dark with a beard, the very thin young boy, Pablo, with the missing finger, who never said anything, and, finally, Eduardo, the tall dark one with the air of authority, who seemed to be in charge of the operation. All of them, except Pablo, wore wedding rings.

There were always two of them on guard, one at the bottom of the stairs by the front door, one outside Bella and Chrissie's door. At night, a guard stayed in their room with a gun ready across his knee.

Ricardo was the most unpleasant. For long periods he'd be quiet, then suddenly get explosive and violently argumentative. Nor did she like the way he stared hungrily at Chrissie.

Diego, on the other hand, was very kind to them. One day, when she was crying, he got out a handkerchief and wiped her eyes. And often, when she got aches and pains from sleeping on the floor, he would rub her back for her. What really frightened her was the pity she frequently detected in his voice. He knows we're going to be killed, she thought in terror.

Physically she felt she was falling to pieces. Her red and white dress was filthy. So was she. She imagined her skin getting covered in blackheads, her eyebrows growing like bushes from not being plucked, her teeth rotting because she couldn't clean them. The stench in the room was terrible. She dreamed obsessively of Lazlo's ivy green bathroom and soaking in hot scented water.

On the fourth night the gunmen started quarrelling amongst themselves. They had been drinking and she could hear them shouting in the room next door. She wished she could understand what they were saying. Chrissie could understand Spanish, but she was asleep.

At midnight Ricardo took over the watch from Diego. He reeked of brandy fumes and stumbled over a loose floorboard. Bella pretended to be asleep.

The shouting died down in the next room and, soon, all was deathly quiet. Bella opened half an eye. In the half light, the gun gleamed across Ricardo's knee. Chrissie turned over and moaned in her sleep, her black hair flopped over her face, the top button of her black dress was undone, showing the marble whiteness of her breasts.

Ricardo's breathing became heavier, as suddenly he got up, stepped over Bella, and went towards the bed. Through half-shut eyes she saw him gazing down at Chrissie's full, voluptuous body, then, very slowly, he put his hand out and began to stroke her face. Chrissie moved again in her sleep, edging towards him, like a dog cuddling up to its owner. Ricardo went on stroking her cheek, then his hand moved slowly down her neck and began to undo the buttons of her dress.

Bella was frozen with horror, unable to move. Suddenly Chrissie woke up and gave a little gasp of terror at the sight of the masked face. Next moment, Ricardo's hand clamped over her mouth and then he was on top of her, clawing at her dress.

Bella reacted instantly.

'Leave her alone,' she yelled, picking up the broken chair, and the next moment she cracked it over Ricardo's head. He gave a groan and collapsed on to the floor as Chrissie started screaming.

Bella was about to hit him again when the door burst open and in came Eduardo, Carlos and Pablo, all carrying guns.

'Put that chair down,' snarled Eduardo.

'He was trying to rape me,' sobbed Chrissie.

Bella, looking at the three gun barrels, dropped the chair. Pablo helped Ricardo to his feet.

'The bitch went for me,' said Ricardo, blood dripping from his head, and the next moment he'd turned on Bella, slapping her viciously across the face, back and forth, back and forth.

'That's enough,' said Eduardo. 'We'll teach her a lesson another way.' He gave instructions in Spanish over his shoulder to Pablo, who went out and came back with some rope with which he tied up both Bella and Chrissie.

They sat Bella down on a chair. She could feel the blood trickling down her cheeks where Ricardo's ring had cut her.

Then Carlos came in with a towel and put it round Bella's shoulders. Suddenly Bella remembered, terrified, how they'd cut off Paul Getty's ear.

'Oh please no!' she whispered.

'Shut up,' said Eduardo, lifting up her hair.

They were all standing behind her.

'No!' screamed Chrissie, 'please don't hurt her.' For she could see what Bella could not, that in Eduardo's hand was a razor blade glinting evilly in the dim light.

Bella jerked her head forward.

'Keep still,' swore Eduardo. 'Or you really will get hurt.'

She felt her hair being tugged backward, and sawed at, this way and that.

'Oh, no!' she wailed. 'Not my hair.'

Eduardo ran the razor blade gently down her cheek.

'Quiet,' he said softly. 'Or we really will give you something to remember us by.'

They cut her long mane off to a ragged three inches all over her head, short as a boy's, shorter than most boys, tugging and sawing till it lay in a heavy mass all over the floor.

Eduardo then told Pablo to gather it up.

'We'll parcel it up and send it to El Gatto. It might make him get off his arse about raising the dough,' said Eduardo.

After that, they took her next door and stood her up, with her hands and feet still tied and her head in a noose of rope hanging from the ceiling.

'Don't fall asleep or the rope will snap your head off,' said Ricardo, and he went out, locking the door.

Bella couldn't stop crying. Her only irrational thought was

that now she'd finally lost Lazlo. She remembered him saying he only liked girls with long hair, not that she'd ever had him. But now, with short hair, there was no possibility that he could love her.

For four nights sleep had eluded her. Now that she had somehow to keep from dropping off, she felt overwhelmed with exhaustion. She *must* keep awake. She tried to remember all the snatches of poetry she had ever known, 'Farewell, thou are too dear for my possessing, And like enough thou know'st thy estimate . . . How like a winter hath my absence been from thee . . . How sad and bad and mad it was, then. But, how it was sweet . . . Oh heart! oh heart! if he'd but turn his head. You'd know the folly of being comforted.'

The trouble with every poem was that it turned her thoughts back to Lazlo, making her re-live the moments they'd spent together. The last time she'd seen him with his back to the fireplace, very suntanned in that dark blue shirt, with strangely softened face, saying, 'Come here,' and her going to him in spite of being frightened, and then the telephone interrupting them just before she reached him.

Then she allowed her thoughts to stray into the dangerous fantasy of the telephone not ringing, of being in his arms and hearing all the lovely things he was saying, his voice husky with passion.

Oh God! she thought, it wasn't the racehorses or the yachts or the fur coats she wanted from him, it was the understanding, the kindness beneath the mocking exterior, the protectiveness he displayed to his family and people he loved.

She started to cry again, overwhelmed by utter despair. Why not fall asleep and die? No! She pulled herself together. Chrissie had to be looked after. They'd got to get out.

Diego took over the watch at four o'clock and was obviously appalled by what he saw.

'My God! What have those bastards done? Your beautiful, beautiful hair.'

He untied the rope round her neck and feet and hands, brushed away the hairs that were itching down her back, and gave her a cigarette.

'What happened?'

She shrugged her shoulders.

'Ricardo tried to rape Chrissie.'

'And?'

'I went for him with a chair.'

'So he had to take his revenge. Is the kid all right?'

Bella nodded. 'Physically anyway. Where are the others?'

'Sleeping. I'll make you a cup of tea.'

He went out, leaving his gun on a chair. Bella could have picked it up and used it, but she felt too tired; and that Diego trusting her was her one chance of getting out. He came back with hot water and soap and washed her face and hands for her. Then he brought her a cup of tea and a pear, which he cut into quarters and peeled for her. Bella had never tasted anything so delicious in her life.

'You're so good to me, Diego,' she said. 'Do I look absolutely hideous like this?'

He shrugged. 'It was prettier long, but it will grow soon.'

'Will I be allowed to live long enough for it to grow?'

'Don't think about things like that. I don't know. I am only given orders.'

She took a gulp of the sweet, scalding tea. It seemed to give her strength.

'Why are you caught up in this racket?' she asked.

'Mine is a very poor country. The only way to make big money in a hurry is on the wrong side of the law.'

Then he told her about his son who was five, who had a very rare heart complaint.

'If he doesn't have an operation soon, he will die. We do not have your health service in my country. Everything has to be paid for. This operation costs a lot of money.

'When this business is all over, and El Gatto pays up, I will have enough to pay for the operation, and be able to take my wife and children to live in a new country. They will arrange a new passport for us.'

'But won't the people who give the orders expect you to do other things for them?'

'No, only one job; that's the deal.'

'But can't you understand the kind of people you're dealing with?' said Bella. 'They'll never let you go once they get their teeth into you. You'll be doing jobs for them for the rest of your life, and one day you'll slip up and it'll be curtains.'

'Shut up,' said Diego. 'It's not true.'

Bella played her trump card.

'Juan Rodriquez is behind this, isn't he?'

Diego started. 'How do you know?'

'Lazlo knows it too, and he's not stupid. It won't be long before he tracks us down and, whether we're dead or alive, you'll have a long, long spell in jug.'

'You're bluffing,' said Diego, suddenly very agitated.

'Juan Rodriguez is hardly the sort of name I'd make up. Look, I know all about him, how powerful and vicious he is. He'll never let you go after one job. And if he bumps off Chrissie and me – which he intends to, doesn't he? – whether they get the cash or not, Lazlo will hunt the lot of you down until he gets his revenge. With two man-eating tigers on your tracks, you'll never get that peaceful life you want with your wife and child.'

Diego got up and began to pace about the room.

Bella's heart was pounding, but she tried to keep her voice calm:

'Look, Diego, I swear something – if you tip Lazlo off where we are, and it'll only take one telephone call, he'll look after you, he'll get your wife out of Buenos Aires, and he'll see your child gets the best medical treatment in the world. And you'll be able to live in peace for the rest of your life, not as a hunted man.'

'You're crazy,' said Diego. 'The Fuzz'll grab me the minute I get out of here.'

'You'll do a year at the most – particularly as it's your first offence – but probably Lazlo'll be able to fiddle it so you don't even do that – and at least your wife will be safe and your little boy saved.'

Diego sat down and picked up his gun and pointed it at her.

'Don't you realize the greatest crime among my people is *infamita*,' he said sternly. 'To talk to the authorities. If I shopped the others, Juan would make sure I was dead in a week.'

'Not if you had Lazlo's protection. They're not worth being loyal to, this lot. They're a bunch of cheap crooks. You're different, Diego. You're a good person, I can tell.'

'Don't talk to me like that. If the others heard you, it

wouldn't be just your hair they'd chop off,' snapped Diego. 'Lie down and get some sleep.' He took off his coat and laid it over her shoulders.

'I ache all over,' said Bella, 'I can't sleep. Rub my back and tell me more about your little boy.'

CHAPTER TWENTY

ANOTHER day and night limped by. Pablo, feeling contrite, perhaps over his part in last night's shearing, gave her an old copy of *Woman's Own* to read. To Bella it was like stumbling on Chapman's Homer. Over and over again she read the cosy hints on crocheting and making lampshades, and the romantic stories with their happy endings. How her mouth watered as she pored over the pictures of Lancashire Hot Pot, and cheap ways with end of neck.

Best of all was being able to look at new faces. Apart from Chrissie, she'd seen nothing but masks for the last five days. But at the back of her mind was always the thought that time was running out, like High Noon. Do not forsake me, oh my darling.

The following morning Pablo was keeping guard in her room, smiling to himself as he polished his gun. Then shouting broke out next door.

'Get on guard,' she could hear Eduardo yelling. 'You know there should be two of you.'

'I need a drink.' It was Ricardo's chillingly oily whine.

'You've had your ration for the day,' snapped Eduardo. 'Go back to your post.'

'I want a drink.'

'There's only half a bottle left.'

'Well, someone's got to go out tomorrow and get some more.'

'It's too dangerous,' said Eduardo's voice, harsh with exasperation.

As the day crawled by, the atmosphere grew more and more tense, quarrels flaring up at the most innocent remarks. Carlos complained Ricardo hadn't put sugar in his tea. Ricardo hit the roof. Eduardo nearly got all the soup poured over him when he suggested there wasn't enough salt in it. If this inaction goes on much longer, thought Bella, they'll be at each other's throats.

At midnight, Diego took over the guard. At first he was offhand, and sullenly refused to talk to her.

'It must be very hot in Buenos Aires now,' said Bella.

Diego took no notice.

'Not much fun for a young mother looking after a sick child,' she went on.

'I don't want to talk about it,' exploded Diego.

'I was brought up in the slums myself,' said Bella. 'And I know what hell it is, and what it's like to escape and leave it all behind.'

'Ending up in a deserted farmhouse with a gun at your head, eh?' said Diego.

'That was just bad luck, but every child deserves a chance to get away, and one's own child most of all. Oh, Diego, don't you *love* him?'

'Of course I do,' he snarled. 'What do you think I did this for?'

'Then give him a chance to get better, and run in the sunshine, and go to a good school, and wear nice clothes.'

'Juan'll give me all that.'

'Rubbish. He's just put a noose round your neck, which he'll tighten if ever you don't play ball and do what he wants. Lazlo Henriques is a good man, whatever you've heard to the contrary,' she went on, her voice breaking slightly. 'He's tough but he knows how to look after his own people.'

'You love him, don't you?' said Diego softly.

Bella nodded, a great lump in her throat. 'And I'll probably never see him again.' The tears ran down her cheeks and she was overwhelmed by such despair that it was a few seconds before she realized what Diego was saying.

'If I contact El Gatto, how will he know I'm on the level?'

Bella's heart leapt. 'You're going to do it?'

'I don't know. Come on, how will he know?'

'I'll write him a note.'

'No, that's too dangerous.'

'Well, have this ring,' she slid the little gold ring studded with seed pearls off her finger. 'Rupert gave it to me. Lazlo always said it was the only thing he'd ever seen me wear that wasn't in appallingly bad taste. And use Black Opal as the password. Those are both private jokes that no one would know anything about. Oh, Diego, you won't regret it, I promise you. Just tell him where we are and how to find us.'

'I haven't made up my mind yet,' said Diego, pocketing the ring.

Suddenly, there was a great crash from next door.

'They're quarrelling again. Probably about you,' said Diego, getting up and going out.

A few minutes later he was back.

'Ricardo's just knocked over the last of the whisky. Carlos slugged Ricardo. Tempers are running high.'

'Then you'll have to get some more supplies tomorrow,' said Bella.

'I don't promise anything,' said Diego.

The next day dawned hotter and more sultry. There were flies everywhere, the stench grew even more terrible. I wonder how nuns survive for years and years without washing, thought Bella. The hair was growing bristly on her legs.

'There'll soon be enough scurf in my hair to bread a veal chop,' she moaned. 'Oh God! I feel horrible.'

Diego's watch was taken over by Eduardo, who brought the wireless with him. At eight came the news. She could feel him tensing himself, but there was again no mention of the kidnapping. Everyone had forgotten them. So much for Lazlo's underworld connections.

When they played pop music, she got up and danced a few steps. Later she listened to *Waggoner's Walk.* It was hard to realize that outside life was going on as usual. People were making love, going to their offices, having toast and marmalade for breakfast.

For her breakfast she had tea without milk and a stale crust of bread.

'Is the service included?' she said.

'What?' said Eduardo.

'Oh forget it,' said Bella.

They were obviously running out of supplies.

About midday there was a lot of talking and whispering outside, and Pablo came in and tied her hands again. She was nervous; she dreaded changes in routine, but they only took her into Chrissie's room.

Chrissie seemed pathetically pleased to see her, but in bad shape.

'How much longer is this going on?' was her first question. 'I'm cracking up.'

'Sssh, something's bound to happen soon.'

'I'll go mad first. Why have they put us together again? They never do anything nice without an ulterior motive. I'm scared when they start softening up.'

'I think they're going off to get supplies, and we're easier to guard if we're both in the same room.'

Someone shouted something in Spanish outside.

Chrissie went pale.

'What are they saying?' said Bella.

'They said "Tell El Gatto if the money isn't raised by midnight tonight, it's curtains".'

'That means they're going to ring Lazlo,' said Bella.

'Oh, God! I know we're going to be killed,' said Chrissie.

Bella did her best to comfort her, but she was really worried by Chrissie's low morale and by her health. Her eyes were sunken, her cheeks were flushed and in spite of the stultifying heat of the day, she was shaking uncontrollably. She had also developed a tight, rasping cough.

She got Chrissie back on to the subject of Rupert, letting her ramble on and on.

Finally Chrissie said, 'I'm talking too much.'

'Talk all you want. There's nothing else we can do.'

'I've had a hell of a lot of time to think in the past twenty-four hours. I've been so vile to you because of Rupert. We all were, but me in particular, shouting at you at the wedding, then bitching you up over the weekend, and finally,' her voice cracked, 'putting the diamond in your suitcase.'

'It doesn't matter,' said Bella. 'If I loved someone, I'd have behaved just the same.'

'But you've been so good to me since I've been here. You're so strong and brave. You say you're ashamed of the kind of background you have, but it certainly makes you able to cope with a situation like this, standing up to them, going for Ricardo with that chair. I don't really know why you're doing it, but I just want to say thank you, and that I was quite wrong about you, and that I really love you, and I'm sorry I've been so bloody.'

Bella turned away so Chrissie wouldn't see she was crying. Ridiculous that when things were so grim, Chrissie saying those things should make her so happy.

'Lazlo's got you all wrong,' said Chrissie, 'and when we – I mean if we – one's so superstitious about presuming anything – get out, I'll tell him how lovely you are.'

She started to cough, on and on, until Eduardo brought her a glass of water.

'You'll have to get her something stronger,' said Bella.

'The others are going to bring back cough medicine,' said Eduardo.

CHAPTER TWENTY-ONE

THE waiting was terrible. Bella read stories from *Woman's Own* out loud, acting out the dialogue, camping it up to make Chrissie laugh. Finally Chrissie fell into an uneasy sleep. It was amazing to Bella that her violent spasms of coughing didn't wake her up.

The two o'clock news still had no mention of the kidnapping, but, as the afternoon passed, Bella began to sense an increasing restlessness amongst the gunmen. Just after four o'clock there was a swift crunch on the gravel, three knocks, the front door opening and shutting, followed by raised, urgent voices.

Chrissie woke up.

'I can't stand it,' she sobbed. 'I can't bear being cooped up any more.'

'Hush,' said Bella sharply. 'I want to listen.'

She could recognize Carlo's thick accent, and Eduardo's deep, authoritative voice, and Ricardo's oily whine, but she couldn't hear Diego's light, gentle drawl. Her palms were soaking; she must keep calm.

The next moment the door was unlocked and in came Ricardo and Eduardo, looking thunderous, and dragged her off into the living-room. Ricardo seized her and forced her arm behind her back, his fingers biting into her flesh.

'You've been talking to Diego, haven't you?' he said. 'Where is he?'

'Ow, you're hurting me,' said Bella, joy bubbling up inside her. 'How should I know where he is? I've been locked up all the time. Isn't he here?'

Ricardo bent her arm even farther back.

'He liked you. He fancied you. You've talked him round.'

'I have not,' said Bella indignantly. 'It's more than my life's worth to talk to anyone here. Where is he?'

'None of your business,' snapped Eduardo.

They cross-questioned her endlessly. Had she talked to Diego? What was his mood last night? Several times they gave her stinging slaps across the face, but she was too elated to care.

Finally she asked if she could have a cigarette.

'We haven't got any,' said Ricardo. 'Diego's done a bunk with all the supplies.'

She was thrown back into the room with Chrissie.

'Don't get too excited, and don't ask me any questions,' she muttered, 'but things are looking up.'

'Tell me,' whispered Chrissie.

'Better if I don't,' said Bella. 'If you don't know, they can't beat it out of you.'

Outside the door she could hear the panicking getting worse. Hope grew inside her. If only they didn't get frightened into becoming violent. She re-read that damn *Woman's Own* over and over again. She could crochet that matinée jacket in her sleep now, but she had to force herself to do something or she'd go nuts.

Hours limped by, waiting for a crunch on the gravel that didn't come. She listened to every bulletin on the wireless, but there was still no reference.

Chrissie's cough was getting worse, and on Bella's nerves. She suddenly started panicking that they'd notice her ring was missing. There was a suntan band where it had gone. Could she say it had dropped off because she'd got so thin and she couldn't find it?

Back came Eduardo and Ricardo to cross-question her.

'What did he talk about last night? Tell us again.'

'Nothing much, mostly about his son. He was worried about his health. Maybe he's telephoned home and got bad news and made a bolt for it.'

'You know something?'

'God, I wish I did. I'd have hitched a lift if I knew he was going to do a bunk.'

'Stop fooling about,' said Eduardo.

'We're going to start cutting bits off you and send them to El Gatto through the post,' said Ricardo evilly.

Chrissie gave a sob.

'He should have got your hair by now,' said Eduardo. 'What

shall we send him next?' He picked up her hand and examined her fingers. For a minute Bella froze with horror, then she realized it wasn't her seed pearl ring hand.

Ricardo was waving a razor, making patterns in the air. Then he ran it down Bella's face.

'Shall Eduardo and I play noughts and crosses?' he said.

'Come on, talk,' snapped Eduardo.

'I don't know anything,' Bella muttered, cringing away from him.

'Talk,' hissed Ricardo.

Suddenly Eduardo stiffened.

'Listen,' he said sharply.

And above the thumping of her heart, Bella could hear a faint droning, like a hoover in a far off room. Then it grew louder, buzzing like an angry wasp, coming nearer and nearer.

A helicopter, thought Bella. Thank God.

It was obviously taking its time, buzzing round and round overhead.

Eduardo swore softly. Both he and Ricardo went out to look. She could hear their anxious voices outside.

'I think,' she said to Chrissie, 'we've been located.'

Pablo came and sat on guard in their room and picked up his book, but Bella noticed he was reading with unnatural slowness, his eyes fixed on the same place. Occasionally his fingers drummed on the back of the book, and he kept darting fearful glances towards the window.

They're rattled, thought Bella joyfully. Really rattled.

Next door she could hear Eduardo gabbling away to Ricardo in Spanish. It was too fast for her.

'What are they saying?' she asked Chrissie.

'They're arguing about whether to make a bolt for it now, or wait until dark,' said Chrissie.

Bella's red and white dress was drenched in sweat. It was impossibly hot. Suddenly there was a flash, followed by a huge clap of thunder, and the storm that had been lingering for days broke over the house. Flash after flash filtered through the boarded-up window. The rain was falling like machine-gun fire on the roof.

People were crashing about next door. Oh God, they're getting ready to move out, thought Bella. Perhaps we haven't been discovered at all. Maybe the helicopter was just a farmer going home, or a politician returning to his constituency. Ricardo, probably for something to do, returned to his taunting and questioning.

'We'll cut off your foot, I think,' he said. 'And send it through the post to El Gatto.'

'Wouldn't go through the letter box,' said Bella. 'Lazlo's always out anyway, so the Post Office'd have to send him one of those buff pieces of paper saying we have tried to deliver this foot several times; why not apply to Knightsbridge Post Office?'

She began to laugh hysterically, then clapped her hands over her mouth. She mustn't crack up, she mustn't.

Ricardo then tied up their hands and took them into the living-room. Everything had been tidied up, a couple of suit-cases packed. Carlos was burning rubbish in the fireplace; Pablo was running a duster all over the furniture to remove the fingerprints.

There was a commercial on the wireless now, a girl's voice crooning about men loving her shining, lustrous hair.

Lucky thing, thought Bella wistfully, remembering her long mane. What would Lazlo think when he got the parcel, she wondered. Would he be sorry, or just think how ugly she must be now? It's what you are – funny, talented, beautiful – that matters. Oh, Lazlo, Lazlo. She felt the tears trickling down her cheeks.

Suddenly her musings were interrupted by the calm impass-ive voice of the news reader.

'News has suddenly come to light of a double kidnapping which began in London nine days ago, when Christine Hen-riques, the niece of Charles Henriques, chairman of Henriques Brothers, the banking firm, was seized as she was leaving her uncle's house in Chelsea. The kidnappers demanded a ransom of two million pounds, but warned the family to raise the money privately and not to notify the police. Three days later, actress Bella Parkinson, who is engaged to Rupert Henriques, the son of Charles Henriques, was also kidnapped on her way home from the theatre, and the kidnappers stepped up the demand.

'Today, however, there was a major break-through when one

of the gang contacted the family with vital information about the whereabouts of the kidnappers and their victims. The men are all believed to be South American, and police have made important steps in tracing the men behind the kidnapping, both in England and South America. The kidnapping is not believed to be motivated by politics.'

There was a long pause, then everyone started shouting and swearing. Bella didn't dare look at Chrissie.

'They'll kill us in a minute,' said Chrissie in a shaking voice.

'I don't think so,' said Bella. 'We're the only card they've got left.'

'I can't stand the tension,' said Chrissie.

'You've got to,' said Bella. 'Don't upset them. All we can do now is wait.'

In the silence between thunder claps they heard the helicopter buzzing round again.

'Come on,' said Eduardo. 'We'd better get the hell out of here.' He put a blindfold over Bella's eyes, tied it tightly. Then she felt herself being led down the stairs.

Oh why doesn't Lazlo hurry, she prayed. If we leave here they'll never find us.

They paused at the bottom of the stairs. Bella could sense the tension around her. The storm seemed to have stopped.

'I'm going outside to see if the coast's clear,' said Carlos. He opened the door and shut it again.

'What's that?' said Ricardo.

There was a crackling and they all jumped at the sound of a loudspeaker.

'You are completely surrounded,' said a voice. 'Throw your guns out of the window. Send Bella and Chrissie out at once, alone and then come out one by one with your hands up. Do not attempt to escape, or you will be shot down.'

'They're bluffing,' said Eduardo. 'I'm going to have a look.' He put his head out of the door.

In answer, a semi-circle of floodlights flashed on, flaring between the trees in an arc nearly a hundred yards long.

'Jesus!' said Carlos. 'We're done for.'

'No we're not,' said Eduardo. 'They won't shoot into the house for fear of killing Bella or Chrissie.'

A policeman moved forward from the lights. The next

moment Eduardo opened up with a machine gun. Then he seized the terrified Chrissie, jammed the smouldering gun in her back and, dragging her upstairs, opened the window.

'Go on,' he hissed, jamming the gun further into her back, 'or I'll pull the trigger. Tell them to go away, that they're not helping, and they've got to do anything we ask.'

'Go away!' screamed Chrissie. 'They'll kill us, they'll kill us.' Her voice dried up on a screeched whisper.

'Tell them they've got to do what we tell them,' whispered Eduardo. 'We want a car to get out of here and a plane to take us to South America. Go on.'

'You've got to do what they tell you,' screamed Chrissie, repeating his message, then breaking down into hysterical coughing and sobbing.

There was total silence.

Eduardo pulled Chrissie inside and shut the window.

They all gathered in the living-room at the back, Bella and Chrissie tied up, Pablo keeping watch at the front, Ricardo with his gun trained on the two girls, Carlos and Eduardo discussing their next move.

Chrissie was still coughing and crying.

'Don't worry,' whispered Bella. 'They can't hold out much longer. It must be over soon.'

Carlos found a further news bulletin on another channel. The kidnapping was again the lead story.

'The hideout of the kidnappers has now beeen discovered,' said the announcer. 'A remote farmhouse just outside Haltby on the Devonshire coast. It has been completely surrounded by the army and the police. Police also know the names of the four kidnappers, and realize they are only the front for a much larger organization. Police and the army now have the whole area cordoned off and are preparing for a long siege.

'A quarter of an hour ago, one of the gang appeared at the front door and shot at the police. Later a gunman held Miss Christine Henriques out of a first floor window at gunpoint. In considerable distress she appealed to the police not to threaten the gunmen and to agree to anything they ask for.'

Chrissie was coughing non-stop now.

'For Christ's sake shut her up,' said Ricardo.

'Why don't you let her go?' said Bella. 'If she gets any worse, you'll have a murder on your hands without trying.'

There was another crackling over the loudspeaker. Another voice was speaking now in fluent Spanish. Bella's heart gave a lurch; she felt blood rushing to her face. It was Lazlo. Chrissie tried to struggle to her feet; Bella gave a gasp of excitement which turned to terror as Ricardo shoved a gun against her temple.

'Leave her alone,' snapped Eduardo, 'and listen. It's El Gatto's voice,' and she could feel the frisson of loathing around the room. These are men, she thought, with a shiver, who have been taught to hate the name Henriques at their mother's knee.

Lazlo's voice went on, softer, more persuasive now. It was too fast for her to follow.

'What's he saying?' she whispered to Chrissie.

'That the police know who all the men are,' said Chrissie. 'And have photographs of them, that there's no way the police are going to give them an aeroplane, or a car.' She listened for a minute, then caught her breath. 'Now he's saying Juan and Steve have both been pulled in, so there's no point them resisting any more. If they surrender they won't be harmed in any way.'

Bella wished she could see the gunmen's faces to see how they were reacting.

The loudspeaker crackled and stopped.

'Finally he said the police were in no hurry and intend to wait until the gunmen saw reason,' said Chrissie.

All very well, thought Bella, but this lot are human time bombs, liable to explode at any minute.

They were arguing violently now.

'Eduardo doesn't believe Juan or Steve have been arrested,' said Chrissie. 'He thinks Lazlo's bluffing. Ricardo agrees with him. Carlos is fed up and all for packing it in. Pablo, as usual, says nothing.'

'They've run out of booze and food and cigarettes,' said Bella. 'They can't hold out much longer.'

'If they get hungry, they'll get bloody-minded,' said Chrissie. 'If they starve them out, there'll be more chance of a shoot-out.'

There was no sound or sign of life from outside. The transistor was crackling like distant gunfire as they waited for the next news bulletin. It was the same as the one before, except it added that the police knew the gunmen had run out of food and drink, and included an interview with a doctor on the effects of long-term starvation.

'It is likely to sharpen the wits, but decrease physical efficiency,' said the doctor in a calm, flat voice.

'Great,' said Bella. 'We'll all be cracking jokes soon.'

'Then the pangs of hunger will give way to dull, painless lethargy, probably accompanied by headaches,' went on the doctor.

'How soon will the hostages be in any physical danger through lack of food?' said the interviewer.

'Man can live without permanent ill effects up to six weeks on water alone,' said the doctor.

'Jesus,' muttered Bella. 'It's a hell of a way to go on a crash diet.'

The voice faded and crackled again when Eduardo shook the wireless. The batteries are running out, thought Bella. She moved slightly. Her side ached where the floor boards were biting into her flesh.

She started on The Lord's Prayer. It was too serious a time to make bargains with God she couldn't keep. Please let me out, she prayed, and I'll try to be good for the rest of my life, and try not to want Lazlo too much if he doesn't want me.

The wind came in a sudden blast, rattling the trees against the roof of the house. Next moment, the arc lights went out.

'This is your chance,' said Carlos.

'They're trying to tempt one of us out,' said Eduardo.

Ricardo tiptoed downstairs and slowly opened the front door. The next moment the lights went on and a volley of bullets was fired over the house.

'Your blackmail has failed,' said the loudspeaker. 'Send the girls out at once if you want to save your lives.'

They heard whispering and breathing on the loudspeaker. Then everything went quiet.

CHAPTER TWENTY-TWO

SOMEHOW it was dawn. It seemed to Bella that they had been left to their fate. She had terrible cramp down her side. The floodlights had lost their brilliance under the door. The loudspeaker had been silent for hours. She had even dozed fitfully. Even Chrissie, having coughed half the night, was asleep, snoring gently, perhaps dreaming of Rupert and her soft bed at home.

Carlos was dozing now, curled up like an embryo. Ricardo guarded the front door still, Eduardo the window. Pablo had his gun trained on her and Chrissie.

How can she sleep so peacefully, Bella wondered.

Eduardo reached out and switched on the transistor, but it spluttered and finally gave out.

They were arguing again now in low voices. Ricardo was obviously the one suffering most; he was desperate for cigarettes and alcohol, his nails bitten down to the quick.

The loudspeaker began again, making them all jump.

'Take the only way out and surrender. Take the only way out.'

'I must go to the loo,' said Bella.

Ricardo looked at Eduardo who nodded tersely. Ricardo undid Bella's legs and, at gunpoint, led her to the lavatory at the end of the passage. For a second, she was able to peer out of a crack between the boarded windows. The sight cheered her up. Across the grass on the edge of a wood she could see rows of policemen, motionless and intent, with revolvers raised to the window. Other policemen moved around behind rows of sandbags. Beyond were television cameras and television catering vans and hundreds of Special Branch men, and handlers with alsatians on leads, eyes alert, tails wagging expectantly.

She strained her eyes to catch a glimpse of Lazlo or Rupert.

'Come on, you've been in there long enough,' said Ricardo.

Feeling slightly dizzy, she stumbled back to the living-room, where Chrissie had just woken up, and realizing where she was, had started the interminable coughing and crying. Bella felt her head; she was boiling hot with temperature.

'Why don't you let her go?' she said, turning furiously on Eduardo. 'You know you're finished.'

Ricardo raised his gun at her.

'Juan will rescue us,' said Eduardo quietly.

'Rubbish,' said Bella. 'Didn't you hear Lazlo saying he'd been arrested, and even if he hadn't been, you know the kind of man he is, that he'd disown you the moment things got awkward.'

'Not me,' said Eduardo, with sudden hauteur, 'Juan would never let me down, nor I him.'

The day began to take on a nightmare quality. Eduardo was constantly having to rally the others as, over and over again, the loudspeaker made offers of food and cigarettes in return for releasing one of the hostages, all of which were refused.

In all the big kidnapping cases Bella had read about recently, the besieged gunmen had eventually capitulated. But this is different, she thought. It's a hatred thing, all tied up with Eduardo's damn *machismo*. He'll never give in without a struggle.

At dusk the lights in the living-room went out. Carlos stumbled out to the hall and tried the light switch there. No light came on. 'They've turned the bloody electricity off,' he shouted.

For several hours they waited, trembling in pitch dark; then, suddenly, brilliant super arc lights blazed into the room, making them all cover their eyes. These lights were switched on, off, on, off, making sleep absolutely impossible. They all moved into one of the boarded-up rooms.

Chrissie seemed to have sunk into a dull torpor, which worried Bella far more than the coughing, sobbing and shivering.

The police are going about it the wrong way, she thought. We're going to crack before the gunmen.

Another dawn slowly reduced the power of the arc lights. Bella had lost the ability to feel anything.

Ricardo and Eduardo and Carlos were all at each other's throats. If they start offering them cigarettes today, thought Bella, Eduardo's going to have the devil's own job stopping them accepting.

The loudspeaker crackled.

Chrissie woke up. 'What's that?' she said listlessly.

'It's Lazlo,' said Bella.

He was talking in Spanish again.

'Tell me what he's saying.'

Chrissie wriggled into a sitting position and listened.

'He says he's got something of particular interest for both Ricardo and Carlos. Ricardo first. He wants them to listen carefully.'

Suddenly there was a woman's voice, pleading, sobbing, beseeching, choking with emotion. Intensified a hundred times by the loudspeaker, it sounded terrible.

Ricardo gave a groan and sat down with his hands over his ears.

'What's she saying?' Bella hissed to Chrissie.

'It's his mother,' said Chrissie. 'She's pleading with him to give himself up and let us go free. She says she's an old woman, and if he gets killed her life will be meaningless and, as she'll never be able to afford to come to England, she'll never see him again. Now she's asking him to think of his sister, who's about the same age as us. Now she's saying that Juan has been arrested, and what are five years in prison, which he'll get if he gives himself up, compared to death when he hasn't even said his confession.'

She finished speaking and started to cry.

Ricardo got to his feet. 'Stop it! Stop it!' he screamed. 'I can't stand it.'

'Pull yourself together,' said Eduardo icily. 'Can't you see she's been forced into doing it.'

'Not my mother,' hissed Ricardo. 'Never! She would never let herself be forced into anything.'

The loudspeaker began again. This time it was Carlos's wife. A quieter, more impassioned plea, asking Carlos to save himself because she and the children loved him, and they wanted him back. Again she told him to remember that Bella and

Chrissie were only young girls who hadn't done anyone any harm.

Carlos reacted in a far less hysterical way than Ricardo, but Bella could tell from his still body and clenched fists that he was very much affected.

Nothing for Eduardo, she thought. Probably no one loved him enough to plead with him to save his life. And what about the mute Pablo, standing motionless beside the door?

There was silence. Then a voice speaking Spanish. Not Lazlo's this time.

'We repeat, come out at once, and throw your guns out. Let the hostages out and come out yourselves, with your hands over your head, and you will not be harmed.'

'Don't take any notice of those lousy tapes,' said Eduardo. 'They're all rigged.'

He sounded calm but the knuckles were white where he clutched his gun.

'I've had enough,' said Ricardo. 'If they've got my mother, they're quite capable of doing things to her. I'm packing it in.'

'So am I,' said Carlos.

Bella felt a surge of hope that died almost immediately.

'No you're not,' said Eduardo, his voice suddenly full of ice. 'We came here to do a job, and we're going to do it. Later Juan will protect us.'

'Not if you're dead, he can't,' said Bella.

'Shut up, you bitch,' snarled Eduardo.

He waved his gun at Ricardo. 'Tie their legs up again,' he said.

Ricardo's hands were shaking so much it took him a long time to tie the knots.

'Now blindfold them.'

'*No*,' said Carlos, starting to argue.

'Go on – blindfold them,' said Eduardo.

And Bella knew it was the voice of the executioner.

Cold fear paralysed her; her throat was completely dry; she wanted to scream for help, to tell them not to kill her, but as the soft scarf was tied over her eyes, she was incapable of speech.

Someone turned her to face the wall.

She heard Eduardo order Pablo to cover the front door with the sub-machine gun, and Ricardo and Carlos to guard the two windows.

'They're going to kill us, aren't they?' whispered Chrissie beside her.

'I'm not sure,' said Bella.

'Will it hurt very much?'

'I don't think so. They say when the wound's mortal, it hurts very little.'

Ricardo was arguing again.

'Shut up,' said Eduardo. 'I'm going to do this. I'll take the complete blame.'

There was a long pause.

No, prayed Bella. Please God, no. She had a sudden vision of Lazlo, of his face softened, holding out his arms to her. Then it seemed to merge with her father with his laughing tawny eyes gathering her up in his arms and holding her, shrieking with delight, above his head. Then she remembered her first night in *Othello*, and the audience clapping and clapping, and the deafening way they'd clapped the night Lazlo had made her go on after the diamond was stolen. And suddenly the deafening applause seemed to turn into a volley of machine-gun fire, and the next moment she heard a groan and a scream as a body slumped at her side.

'Chrissie,' she screamed. 'You've killed her, bastards, bastards.'

She tensed herself waiting for another volley of shooting, but it never came. Suddenly the blindfold was removed from her eyes. She looked down at Chrissie lying at her feet, expecting her to be full of holes, and realized with sudden, incredulous joy, that she was still breathing.

Hardly daring to turn her head, she suddenly saw a trickle of blood coming down the floorboards towards her feet. It slowly impinged on her half-crazed mind that it was Eduardo lying dead, riddled with bullets.

And now Pablo was talking for the first time, in a young, hoarse voice, telling Ricardo to throw all the guns out of the window.

Cautiously Ricardo opened the window, ducking to avoid a spurt of machine-gun fire from the ground, and then threw two guns out. The firing started for a second, then died away. Ricardo picked up the remaining guns and threw them out.

Bella managed to bring Chrissie round, while Carlos was untying her ropes.

'What happened?' she gasped.

'You fainted,' said Bella. 'Pablo shot Eduardo. They're just throwing their guns out.'

Hope sparked in Chrissie's dull, bloodshot eyes.

But Pablo still held the machine gun. The next moment he shoved it into Bella's back, making a gesture towards the stairs with his head.

'Out you go,' he said.

She had to support Chrissie down the stairs; she seemed very frail; she must have lost pounds. Pablo came to the door with them, still clutching his gun.

Bella turned to them, 'It's a trick,' she said. 'You'll shoot me in the back.'

Pablo shook his head.

'Why did you shoot Eduardo?'

'To prevent him shooting you,' said Pablo. 'He had to, you see. He couldn't give in like the rest of us. It was a matter of honour. He's Juan's youngest brother.'

Then he opened the door and threw his smoking gun on to the grass.

'Thank you,' said Bella. 'I'll tell them you saved our lives.'

He gave a crooked smile, stood back, and with a curious mock salute, ushered her out on to the grass.

For a minute she was dazzled by the brilliant sunlight, and then the world came back to her in sharp focus. Fifty yards of parched grass stretched out before her. To her left the guns lay in a pile like spillikins. Beyond the grass, the trees and the sandbags began.

It was deadly quiet. There was no one in sight. A dog barked on the left.

Bella walked slowly and hesitantly on, half carrying the stumbling, trembling Chrissie, tensing her backbone against a possible bullet.

She was only a few yards from the shadow of the trees now, and she realized once more the strength of the operation – the dog handlers, the armoured cars, the television cameras, the ambulances, the hordes of policemen. Next moment she had reached the sandbags and collapsed into the arms of a waiting policeman, feeling his silver buttons against her chest, and a hundred arms seemed to be pulling them both to safety behind the sandbags. Then there were people all round her, and photographers flashing and cameras whirring.

And suddenly there was Lazlo, and she hardly recognized him. She had remembered him catlike, sunburnt, exotic-looking in that white suit. Now he was deathly pale, unshaven, his face seamed with exhaustion, his eyes bloodshot, his jaw quilted with muscles to stop himself breaking down.

'Oh Lazlo,' sobbed Chrissie, and collapsed, coughing and sobbing, into his arms.

'It's all right, baby,' he said shakily. 'It's all over. You're going to be all right. You're safe now.'

Over her shoulder, his eyes met Bella's.

'Everything's all right now,' he repeated mechanically.

The next moment, like a dog that's been deprived of its master's company for days, a figure threw himself on Chrissie, tugging her away from Lazlo, cradling her in his arms, kissing her face over and over again. 'Oh my darling, my only love.'

It was Rupert.

'You're all right? You're not hurt?' he went on, pausing and looking down at her.

Chrissie started to laugh and cry at the same time.

'I'm all right, but I'm so dirty and horrible and revolting.'

'You're not, you're not; you're mine and you're lovely.'

Bella turned her head away to stop herself breaking down. And then Lazlo was beside her, and she was overwhelmed with shyness. For a moment, as the crowd pushed him forward and he held her tight against him, she could feel his shirt drenched with sweat and the frantic thudding of his heart. Then she pulled away. There were so many people around and she was so filthy and stinking, and she was so ashamed of her terrible hair. She had rehearsed this reunion with him so long, and now she couldn't say anything because she was so terrified of saying too much.

'Chrissie,' she blurted out. 'She's ill. You must get her to a hospital.' She swayed. Lazlo caught hold of her. Then everyone was round her, offering congratulations. A senior policeman in a peaked hat fought his way through the crowd.

'Thank God you're safe,' he said. 'What's happening in there?'

'It's quite safe,' said Bella. 'They've thrown out all their guns.'

'Are they all alive?'

'Three of them. Eduardo's dead. Pablo killed him because he was going to shoot us.'

'Do you feel up to answering a few questions?' said the Inspector.

Bella nodded. 'But I don't think Chrissie ought to; she needs a doctor at once.'

'And how's my star attraction?' said a voice in her ear.

Bella swung round, and there beside her was the wonderfully familiar freckled face of Roger Field.

'Oh, Roger,' she said, her control snapping, and, sobbing, she flung her arms round his neck.

CHAPTER TWENTY-THREE

THEY had to fight their way out. Photographers were snapping frenziedly, journalists pressing forward, but a row of policemen made a gangway, and the next moment, she, Lazlo and Roger were bundled into a police car and driven off.

She clutched on to Roger all the way, shaking uncontrollably, still feeling hopelessly shy of Lazlo who was sitting beside her. Two other policemen in the car inhibited her even further.

Speechless, she gazed out of the window at the countryside she thought she would never see again – at the angelic greenness of the trees, the wild roses hanging in festoons from the banks, the buttercups golden in the fields. Every time a car passed them coming from either direction, she ducked down. She couldn't get used to the fact that no one was pointing a gun at her any longer.

'How's everyone in the company?' she said to Roger.

'Worried stiff about you.'

'I was quite worried myself.' Her laugh wasn't quite steady enough. She half turned to Lazlo. 'Is Diego all right? He got through to you?'

Lazlo nodded.

'And his wife and little boy?' said Bella.

'They're being flown over here tomorrow or the next day. I've alerted all the right people at Great Ormond Street, they'll get the best attention.'

'Oh I am pleased.' She still couldn't look him straight in the eye. 'It wasn't too much of a problem? You didn't mind my saying you'd do that for him?'

'Christ no,' said Roger. 'It was the best hand you've ever played darling. You obviously knocked him for six. I said to Lazlo it's the old Parkinson sex appeal working again.'

She started to laugh, but it strangled in her throat and she started to cry. Roger squeezed her hand harder:

'It's all right, sweetheart. We all know what you've been through. Give her a slug from your hip flask, Lazlo.'

At the police station there were incredible mob scenes: people standing on each other's shoulders, hundreds of reporters and television cameras: 'Let me look at her.' 'That's the girl friend.' 'Look at her hair.' 'Good old Bella.' 'What was it like?' 'Did they hurt you?'

They were all trying to touch her, pulling at her clothing.

Four policemen hustled her inside, where she was allowed to have a cup of coffee and a wash before they started interrogating her. The room was absolutely jammed with cops firing questions from all sides. Roger sat beside her, holding her hand tightly, de-fusing the whole thing when it became over-emotional. Lazlo seemed temporarily to have disappeared.

When they got on to the shooting, she started trembling again.

'You're sure it was Pablo who shot Eduardo?' said the Superintendent.

'Yes, of course.'

'But you were blindfolded,' said an Inspector with a big moustache.

'I could tell from the direction the shots came from,' said Bella. 'And besides, he was the only one with a machine gun.'

'But at first you thought it was Eduardo who had shot Chrissie.'

'I know, but only because I was expecting it.'

'And two machine guns were thrown out of the window.'

'Well they were only using one at the time, and I *know* it was Pablo because he'd been so retiring up until then. Then suddenly he took charge.'

'But you didn't actually see him fire the shot?' persisted the Superintendent.

The possibility that they might not believe she was speaking the truth became too much for her. Suddenly they seemed indistinguishable from Ricardo and Eduardo slapping her face back and forth to get information out of her.

'It's worse out than in,' she said, and laying down her head on the table, she started to cry. 'I'm not up to it. I'm simply not up to it.'

Next moment Lazlo walked in. He had shaved and put on a clean shirt, and seemed to be his old forceful self once again.

'If you don't get off her back,' he said, walking over to the Superintendent, 'I'll make the most bloody awful scandal that'll destroy any public image you've built up over this case.

'It's all right, lovey,' he added, taking Bella's other hand. 'It won't take much longer,' and with infinite tact and gentleness, he took her over the morning's happenings.

'And that's enough,' he said, when she had finished. 'I've just seen my sister. She's not as ill as all that. She'll be perfectly able to give you her story later in the day if you're capable of showing a little consideration.'

The Superintendent shot Lazlo a look both of dislike and respect.

'All right, Mr. Henriques,' he said.

'I'd like somewhere where Miss Parkinson and I can have two minutes alone, together,' Lazlo went on. 'Then you can take her straight to hospital.'

They were ushered into an ante-room with a table and two chairs, which smelt of furniture polish and chalk and fear. A potted plant was wilting on the window ledge.

Bella collapsed on to one of the chairs. 'I don't want to go to hospital,' she said in a shaking voice. 'I'm quite all right.'

'It's only for a check-up, so you can catch up on some sleep. Not for long, only for a day or two until I get back.'

She looked up in horror.

'Where are you going?'

He paused, his face inscrutable.

'Buenos Aires.'

'Oh no! So they were bluffing. Juan hasn't been pulled in yet.'

'Not yet. But I've got all the evidence I need to nail him – and the Argentinian police aren't going to let a chance like this slip through their fingers. So I'll get every co-operation.'

'What's happened to Steve?' she said, and felt herself going crimson.

'Inside,' said Lazlo flatly. 'He was picked up yesterday, trying to leave the country.'

'And he talked?'

Lazlo nodded. 'Straight away, sang to the roof-tops.'

Bella winced. Wretched Steve, not even the guts to protect his own crooked friends.

'He and Juan had been planning to snatch Chrissie for months,' Lazlo went on.

'So contacting me through the personal columns, and pretending to be still madly in love with me . . .'

'Was just a ruse,' said Lazlo. 'He read about you and Rupert in the papers, and went through all the personal column palaver, just to lull your suspicions. He realized how cliquey we are as a family, how we resist outsiders. You were the ideal way in.'

It came out more brutally than he had intended.

'Oh God,' said Bella, feeling suddenly defeated. 'So it was all my fault.'

'Of course it wasn't,' said Lazlo irritably.

There was a knock and a policeman's head came round the door. 'You're going to miss that plane Mr. Henriques, unless you hurry.'

'Just coming,' said Lazlo. 'Give me a few seconds more.'

The head retreated. Bella was staring listlessly at her hands. For a moment it seemed even Lazlo was at a loss for words.

The tension between them was unbearable. She felt an appalling urge to collapse, sobbing in his arms, pleading with him not to go, but she just went on gazing at her bitten nails.

'Bella,' he said gently, 'please look at me.'

'I can't,' she said in a stifled voice. There was another agonizing pause. He sighed and stood up.

'All right, I suppose it's no good trying to sort anything out at the moment. You're all in. Roger'll look after you. Get as much rest as you can. I'll ring you from B.A. as soon as I've got anything to report.'

'You will be careful, won't you?' she said, still not looking up.

'I'll try,' he said wearily, and was gone. And Bella was overwhelmed with a terrible sense of anti-climax.

CHAPTER TWENTY-FOUR

THEY released her after forty-eight hours in hospital. The doctors said she must have an extremely strong constitution. Apart from the fact that at night she was continually woken by nightmares about guns pointing at her, and by day she thought obsessively about Lazlo, she seemed to have made an excellent recovery. Roger steered her through a gruelling press conference when she came out.

The questions about the actual kidnapping and living with the gunmen were bad enough, but soon they moved on to her private life.

'You were engaged to Rupert Henriques,' said the gossip writer from the *Daily Mail*.

'Yes,' said Bella.

'But you broke it off,' he persisted.

'Yes.'

'Why?'

'Because we weren't suited.'

'Or because you were more suited to his cousin, Lazlo?'

'No!' said Bella, going scarlet.

'Lazlo tried to cut his cousin out with you, didn't he?'

'This is *not* a court of law,' said Roger Field, firmly. 'So will you stop pestering Bella with irrelevant questions.'

But throughout the press conference, journalist after journalist harked back to the question of her and Lazlo, until suddenly she lost her temper.

'Will you stop hounding me,' she screamed. 'There is absolutely nothing between Lazlo Henriques and me, and I'm not answering any more of your bloody questions.'

It took all Roger Field's tact to calm everyone down.

'In considerable distress,' wrote down the journalists in their shorthand notebooks, as a minute later Bella suddenly stood up, burst into tears and fled out of the room.

'I can't stand any more,' she sobbed to Roger.

'You won't have to,' said Roger.

Five minutes later she and Roger were smuggled out of a side door and into a waiting police car.

'Where are we going?' said Bella.

'To a bolt hole of Lazlo's in Maida Vale,' said Roger. 'He's been hiding out there since you and Chrissie were kidnapped. Too many people, including the Press, know the address of his own flat.'

They were welcomed at the flat by Roger's wife, Sabina. She was a tall, slim brunette and her beauty in the flesh and in the photograph on Roger's desk at the theatre had blighted the hopes of many a young actress who would otherwise have set her cap at Roger. She gathered Bella into a voluptuous scented hug.

'Welcome home, darling. This flat has to be seen to be believed. I'm sure it's where Lazlo keeps his first eleven mistresses, all that peach-coloured satin and mirrors in the bedroom.'

'Nonsense,' said Roger sharply. 'Lazlo bought it as a base for visiting clients. It merely happens to be empty at the moment because no one's over here. The Arabs go wild about that bedroom.'

'Business must be disintegrating,' said Sabina. 'He hasn't been near the office for days. A huge pile of mail arrived this morning that hadn't been opened since before you were kidnapped. I've put it all in his bedroom. I've put you in there, too, Bella, so you can lie in bed all night and admire your reflection against peach-coloured satin, in the mirror on the ceiling,' she added, carrying Bella's suitcase into the room on the right. Several of Lazlo's sweaters lay on an armchair and on the dressing-table were jumbled together cuff-links, nail scissors, bottles of aftershave, ivory hair brushes, ties, cheque books, a wallet, several race cards, a fountain pen, a huge stack of mail and a pile of five pound notes.

Bella sniffed one of the bottles of aftershave – it had strong overtones of lavender and musk, and immediately conjured up the old smooth, opulent, mocking, self-assured Lazlo she knew before the kidnapping, not the pale, trembling, shattered man who'd greeted her on her escape.

It was almost as though Sabina read her thoughts.

'I don't know how Lazlo survived the last ten days,' she said. 'He never went to bed, working flat out trying to trace you – and not getting a lead from anyone. Just those damn telephone calls at twenty-four hour intervals, getting more and more threatening. Then those absurd tapes they sent to prove that you were still alive, that might have been made any time.'

She took off the fur counterpane from the bed and began folding it up.

'Then your hair arrived through the post. That was the last straw. He was convinced you were both dead. He completely broke down. It's always much worse when someone you never think will, does. Roger thought he was finished. Then, just as he was trying to cheer him up, the telephone rang and it was Diego. After that he was all right.'

Bella felt herself going scarlet. More than anything in the world she wanted to ask Sabina what Lazlo felt about her – but she was too frightened of getting a negative answer.

'I wish he'd ring,' she said for the hundredth time.

'Oh, he'll be all right,' said Sabina. 'He's a cat with ninety-nine lives. I'll leave you to get yourself sorted out. I'm going to cook supper. Come and have a drink when you're ready.'

After she'd gone, Bella looked at herself in the mirror. God, she hated her hair. She wondered if it would be worth getting a wig. She sniffed the aftershave again and felt a sudden spasm of lust and longing. Then, with a beating heart, she started to leaf through the unopened mail. Halfway down she found what she was dreading – a letter from France in a blue airmail envelope with the address written in violet ink in a flowing, expansive hand.

The name on the back was, of course, Angora's. Trust the silly bitch to use violet ink. Bella was itching to open it. It was dated nine days ago, so, probably, Angora didn't even know of the kidnapping when she'd written it. Firmly, Bella put it at the bottom of the pile. Then she changed into a green and black dress. It was in the style of a cheongsam with a high neck – and a slit skirt.

'That's more like the old Bella,' said Roger appreciatively when she went into the drawing-room.

'I feel very un-Gaysha,' she said, 'and what the hell am I going to do about my bloody hair?'

'I rather like it,' said Roger. 'It brings out the latent fag in me. I've decided the next thing you're going to do is Viola.'

' "She never told her love, but let concealment, like a worm i' the bud, feed on her damask cheek",' quoted Bella. 'Sounds just like me.'

After dinner, at about ten o'clock when, for the first time that evening, Bella was not wondering when Lazlo was going to ring, the telephone rang. Roger answered. Suddenly his face relaxed into a smile.

'You're O.K. Great, well done. Well, that's for the best under the circumstances. He won't bother anyone any more. Do you want to talk to Bella?' He handed her the receiver. 'It's Lazlo.'

Her heart was cracking her ribs, her throat was so dry she could hardly speak.

'Oh thank God, you're not hurt.'

'Not a scratch. Everything's sorted out this end.'

'Oh I'm so glad. What about Juan?'

'He's dead. He tried to shoot his way out and wounded a policeman, so they let him have it.'

'God, how horrible!'

'It wasn't very nice. But at least now he's dead a lot of people in Buenos Aires will have their first decent night's sleep in years.

'Look, I can't talk very long, I'm catching a plane in a few minutes.'

'What time do you get into Heathrow?'

'About ten-thirty tomorrow, flight B.725.'

'Shall I meet you?' (Oh God! She could have bitten her tongue off. He probably had half London meeting him, and there she was, forcing herself on him.)

But he merely said, 'Yes, please, and could you ask Roger to ring Diego and say I'm bringing his wife and the child with me, so they had better have an ambulance waiting at the airport.'

'Oh that's sensational,' cried Bella. 'He'll be so pleased. Have a quick word with Roger. I'll see you tomorrow.'

She handed the receiver back to Roger and went into the bedroom and sat down on the bed, burying her burning face in her hands. Oh I love him, I love him, she said to herself. I'll never be able to live through the next twelve hours. In a dream she started wondering what to wear to the airport. Perhaps Sabina would lend her a big hat, but then the brim would get in the way when Lazlo kissed her. Stop it, she said to herself, you're counting your chickens before they're even laid.

Roger came into the bedroom.

'Well, that's nice isn't it?' he said, grinning. 'Good old Lazlo. Rosie Hassell's in a play on I.T.V. in a minute. Do you want to come and watch her?'

'I'm just going to wash my hair first,' said Bella.

After she'd washed it, she went back into the bedroom to comb it into some sort of shape. She was still walking on air. She looked at the mail on the dressing table again. Suddenly, she felt so relaxed, although she knew she shouldn't, she couldn't resist having a read of Angora's letter. With wet fingers she tore open the envelope, and skimmed through the contents. Pandora's Box! Suddenly she gave a gasp of horror and her hand went to her cheek as she read it again properly.

'My darling, darling Lazlo,' every word burnt into her soul. 'Christ, this movie is a bore . . . the director, the producer, the first assistant, have never stopped trying to bang me. The leading man, on the other hand, is trying to bang the first assistant – but that's movies for you. The director is also determined to have a scene in which I take off all my clothes, but so far I've resisted it, keeping myself on toast for you darling.

'I tried to get you on the telephone, but there was no answer, but filming should be finished by the 12th,' that's today, thought Bella numbly, 'and I plan to fly home on the 13th. I hope you've at last managed to extract Bella from Rupert. You should have no difficulty in getting her to transfer her affections to you but what a drag it must have been.

'Anyway, I'll make it up ten thousand times when we meet. All my love and anticipation, Angora.'

Bella started to cry very quietly. So that really was the truth, she said to herself. As she'd been frightened all along, Lazlo had only been paying her so much attention, deliberately to make her fall in love with him, turning the full searchlight beam of his notorious sex appeal on her, just to make sure she'd never go back to Rupert. Well, he'd won all round. She *had* fallen for him, she could never go back to Rupert. Anyway, Rupert had Chrissie now, as Lazlo had always intended. Now he'd achieved his object, he could go back to Angora, who was one of his own kind.

In agony she remembered the Henriques family motto with which Lazlo had taunted her with the first time they'd met, 'Scratch a Henriques and you draw your own blood.'

Where could she go? Where could she escape to? Then suddenly she decided to go back to Nalesworth, the slum where she'd been born. Perhaps there she might find some kind of peace.

Roger and Sabina were well stuck into the play. She scribbled a quick note to Lazlo.

'Dear Lazlo, I'm afraid I snooped and opened this letter of Angora's. It's explanatory really. I'm sorry I've been such a bother to you all. I haven't got any money, so I've borrowed fifty pounds. I'll send it back to you when I've got it. Thank you for getting me out. With my love, Bella.'

Stuffing the fivers into her bag, she pinched a pair of dark glasses and tiptoed out of the flat.

Later, shivering with misery, cold and exhaustion, she crept into an empty carriage and cried without stopping until the train cranked its way into Leeds station.

CHAPTER TWENTY-FIVE

THE flowers on the graves were spattered with mud and bent in the harsh, bleak wind. Bella stood shaking, still in her green and black cheongsam, her teeth chattering, the rain trickling down her neck, and looked down at the lichened tombstone over her mother's grave.

'Bridget Figge, died 1969 – a saint and deeply loved,' said the inscription.

She was a right bitch, thought Bella, and not at all deeply loved by me. Still, she reflected, she might have been different if she hadn't married my poor feckless father. Then she started thinking about Lazlo. And she looked beyond the dark yews of the churchyard at the grey houses and the grey stone walls and the set grey faces of the passers by. This is home, she thought, and I don't like it one bit. I'm going back to London.

When she got on the train, she headed straight for the bar. The commercial travellers and the men in tweed suits around her, were trying to steer Brown Windsor soup into their mouths. It was only after her fourth double gin and tonic that she realized she hadn't eaten properly since last night. By then it seemed too late to start. She ordered another drink. It was funny to see her face on the front of everyone's newspaper, with short shaggy hair and frightened eyes.

'Ten Days of Terror Take Their Toll,' said one headline. 'Bella cracks up during Press conference and denies romance,' said another.

She shrunk further behind her dark glasses, took a slug of gin, and went back to brooding over Lazlo. His behaviour towards her had never been remotely lover-like. In fact, most of the time it had been quite abominable, and yet, and yet, her thoughts kept straying back to the first time he had pretended to be Steve and nearly raped her in the dark. He must have felt something to kiss her like that, and also the way he'd broken down when they sent him her hair.

Everything suddenly became quite simple. She would find Lazlo as soon as she got to London and have it out with him.

By the time she came off the train, she was very drunk indeed. She tottered down the platform, reeling round porters and oncoming luggage trucks. She had great difficulty in finding a telephone booth.

Someone picked up the telephone in Lazlo's Maida Vale flat on the first ring, but it wasn't Lazlo. It sounded like a policeman.

'He's at the office,' said a voice. 'But who's that calling?' Bella didn't answer. 'Who is that calling?' said the voice again with some urgency.

Bella put the receiver down and rang Lazlo's office where she was told Lazlo was in a meeting, but who should they say called. Again the same urgency. Bella rang off.

Suddenly, the fact that Lazlo was somewhere in London was too much for her. I'm going to rout him out, she said to herself.

In the taxi she tried to tidy herself up a bit. Her dress was still soaking wet from the rain, her cheeks were flushed, her eyes glittering. She managed to put eye-shadow on one eye, then got bored and gave up, and emptied the remains of a bottle of scent over herself. She kept rehearsing what she was going to say to him.

Now look here . . . it began.

The taxi got lost three times, but finally drew up outside a vast, tall grey building. Over a sea of bowler hats, Bella read the letters: Henriques Bros.

'Eureka,' she shouted, falling out into the street, and belting through the front door into the building.

The beautiful red-headed receptionist looked at her in fascinated horror.

'Have you come to collect something?' she said slowly.

'Only Lazlo Henriques,' said Bella, tugging her rain sodden skirt down over her bottom.

'Have you got an appointment?'

'No, but it's terribly important I see him,' said Bella, trying to keep the mounting despair out of her voice.

The receptionist caught her first fumes of gin, her cold blue eyes flickered over Bella's stomach.

'Oh gosh, I'm not pregnant,' she gasped. 'Not a bit, in fact, if that's what you're thinking.'

A man in a commissionaire's uniform came out of the lift. The receptionist beckoned to him.

'This – er – person insists on seeing Mr. Lazlo.'

The Commissionaire looked at Bella, then started.

'My Goodness, it's Miss Parkinson isn't it?'

'Yes, yes,' said Bella. 'I must see him, you can't throw me out.' Her voice was rising hysterically.

Suddenly a nearby door opened and a red-faced man came out.

'Can't you stop this damned row, Heywood?' he said.

'Sir, it's Miss Parkinson,' said the commissionaire.

Bella staggered towards the red-faced man. Suddenly, her self-control snapped. 'Please, oh please,' she sobbed, 'I must see Lazlo. You've got to help me.'

Then, over his shoulder, through the haze of cigarette smoke, she looked into a room and saw a long, polished table, and her eyes travelled down two rows of flushed distinguished looking faces, to the man lounging at the end, whose face was as white as theirs were pink. Her heart lurched into her mouth. It was Lazlo.

'Bella,' he roared, getting to his feet and striding down the room. 'Where the bloody hell have you been? I've got half London looking for you.'

'I went to Yorkshire, but it was raining, so I came back again.'

She was beginning to feel very peculiar. Lazlo caught her as she swayed.

'You're drunk,' he said accusingly.

'Horribly, horribly drunk, and horribly, horribly in love with you,' she mumbled and passed out cold in his arms.

CHAPTER TWENTY-SIX

THE first thing that hit her eyes when she woke up was brilliant scarlet wallpaper. She winced, shut her eyes and opened them again quickly and took in the row of ivory hair brushes, the photographs of racehorses on the dressing-table and the rows and rows of suits in the wardrobe. No one else in the world had as many suits as that. She was back in Lazlo's old flat.

She levered herself out of bed and stood on a fur rug, feeling sick. She was wearing a pair of black pyjamas that were far too large for her. She stumbled into the drawing-room. Lazlo was sitting in an armchair watching racing on television and drinking champagne. He looked up and smiled.

'I feel dreadful,' she said, cringing with embarrassment.

He got up and turned down the television sound and poured her a Fernet Branca.

'Ugh – I couldn't drink anything,' she said.

'Shut up and drink it.'

Grumbling she obeyed.

'I'm going to clean my teeth,' she muttered and shot into the bathroom.

As the pounding in her head began to subside, she started to piece the events of the previous day together. She went back into the drawing-room.

'I'm sorry,' she said in a small voice.

'What about?'

'Barging into your office like that. Did I do anything awful?'

'You declared passionate love to me in front of my entire board of directors, and then passed out like a light.'

'Oh God! Were they very shocked?'

'Riveted I should think. There hasn't been anything half so exciting since decimalization.'

'W-what happened then?'

'Oh, I brought you back here.'

'What time is it?' she muttered.

'Nearly ten past three. I was just about to watch the three-fifteen.'

'I'm sorry about being in your bed ... and things. What happened to my clothes? I mean did we ...' she blushed scarlet. 'Er – did we?'

'No we didn't. You were dead to the world and I've never been keen on necrophilia.'

He was laughing at her now.

'I can't help it,' she said sulkily, scuffing the carpet with her feet. 'I didn't mean to behave badly or fall in love with you. It wasn't on the agenda at all. Particularly when you're probably aching to be rid of me, and rush off to Paris on some loathsome, dirty weekend with Angora. All my love and anticipation indeed – the foxy cow.'

Lazlo laughed. 'Bella, darling,' he said. 'You should learn not to open other people's letters. That was Angora's letter to me, not mine to her.'

Then he got to his feet, crossed the room and took her in his arms. Then he bent his head and kissed her very gently. His mouth tasted cool, and faintly of champagne, and halfway through, Bella joined in and kissed him back and the whole thing became extremely ungentle.

Then he said, 'Now, do you still think I'm aching to be in Paris with Angora?'

Bella said she didn't and he kissed her again.

Then he sat down on the sofa and pulled her on to his knee and said:

'Christ, I've been wanting to do that since the night we played murder.'

'Why didn't you, then?'

'I couldn't. I was in one hell of a position. I'd played you a rotten trick, quite deliberately setting out to seduce you by pretending I was Steve. I knew you loathed my guts, I couldn't just move in. One false move would have sent you scuttling back to Steve. But suddenly the biter was well and truly bit. I had to go on seeing you, not because I wanted to take you away from Rupert, but because I simply couldn't keep away.'

'But after Chrissie was kidnapped, you didn't come near me, didn't even ring me up.'

'That was different. Once Juan knew I was hooked on you, I was scared stiff he'd grab you too, as he did in the end. That's why I kept my distance, but I kept tabs on you. You were being followed all the time. Unfortunately, the night they picked you up, the man trailing you had nipped into a café to get some cigarettes. By the time he'd caught up, it was too late. All he saw was you being bundled into a car and driven off. He didn't even get the number plate.

'Jesus, darling, if you knew what I went through those five days when I didn't know where you were. I was so terrified they'd kill you before I had a chance to tell you I loved you. It became an absolute obsession to tell you. I was worried stiff about Chrissie, but the thought of losing you was what was really crucifying me.'

'I was the same,' said Bella. 'The whole time I was in there I thought about you. It was the only thing that kept me sane. I kept dreaming what would happen if I got out and by some miracle we ever did get together. I rehearsed coming out so often, and what I was going to say to you.'

Lazlo picked up her hand and held it against his cheek:

'Oh so did I, so did I,' he sighed. 'And then there was that terrible volley of shooting, and I thought you must be dead, then suddenly you and Chrissie came out. And I lost my nerve. I couldn't do it, I couldn't tell you I loved you in front of all those hordes of people. In case you weren't ready for it, in case you still hated me.'

'And what about rotten Angora and that letter she sent you?'

Lazlo grinned ruefully.

'I'll admit in the beginning I set out to seduce you because I didn't want you to marry Rupert (now I realize it was because I wanted you for myself) so I lined up Angora to get her off with Steve and promised to give her a weekend in Paris if you actually broke it off with Rupert. Well, I don't mind paying for her weekend, but she'll have to find another man to spend it with.'

Bella blushed.

'How's Chrissie?'

'Fine, coming out of hospital today. Rupert won't let her out of his sight.'

'So all your plans have materialized,' said Bella, unable to keep the slight edge out of her voice.

'Not quite,' said Lazlo, tipping her gently off his knee and going over and turning off the television.

'I think just this once I'll miss the three-fifteen.'

Bella nervously cast around for something to say.

'I'm sure Rupert and Chrissie will be very happy,' she said.

'And me? Do you think I'll make you happy?' said Lazlo, moving towards her deliberately and taking her in his arms.

'I know I look sexually experienced,' she mumbled, in panic, 'but I'm not really, not a bit.'

'You don't look as experienced as you might think,' he said softly. 'But we can have the first lesson right now.'

'Oh darling,' she said, burying her face in his shoulder. 'Don't joke about it.'

Careful, she thought, careful. Don't give in straight away. Oh dear, I shouldn't succumb so easily, was her last coherent thought.

So here I am in bed, she said to herself a couple of hours later, and I should be in heaven. Why do I feel as though I want to cut my throat?

'What's the matter?' said Lazlo.

Bella gazed down at her hands.

'I was thinking that now you've had me, you won't want me any more,' she said in a small voice.

'Bella, you have the faith of a gnat,' he said.

'Oh please don't be angry,' she said. 'I want to believe you love me, but you've had such millions and millions of women.'

'I'm glad you put that in the past tense,' he said. He lit a cigarette, inhaled deeply and handed it to her.

Then he said, 'Look, let's get married.'

Bella choked on the cigarette. Then she lay motionless not daring to say anything. He was joking, he must be joking.

'Well you don't seem frightfully enthusiastic,' he said.

'I thought you weren't very keen on marriage.'

'I'm not, in the general run of things. I've never wanted to get married before; never thought it was quite me, going out to dinner every night with the same person. But about you, somehow I feel completely different. I'm scared stiff to let you out of my sight ever again.'

'What about Maria Rodriguez?'

'That was a boy-girl Romeo and Juliet thing. It would never have lasted. What screwed me up was her getting acid thrown in her face and doing herself in.

'I love you, you crazy child,' he went on, taking her face in his hands. 'I'm turned inside out by you. I haven't been so hooked on anyone since I fell in love with the cricket captain at Eton.'

Bella giggled and looked, and saw that although he smiled, the tarmac black eyes were filled with a tenderness that made her quite dizzy.

'Oh please,' she said. 'If you really mean what you said about marriage, I should like it very very much, and could we do it very soon?'

'I'll get a licence tomorrow,' said Lazlo. 'I'm a great believer in bolting the stable door once the horse is well and truly in. And I'm going to ask Roger to give you a sabbatical, so that after we get married, I can take you on a long, long honeymoon, so we can both stop having nightmares about Juan.'

'Oh God,' said Bella with a sob, flinging her arms round his neck. 'I must have done something amazingly good in a former existence to deserve this.'

'You did something amazingly good during the last couple of hours,' said Lazlo, and he kissed her again.

'Another nice thing,' he said, when he finally came up for air, 'is that Aunt Constance will be insane with rage.'

Bella giggled again, then she suddenly caught sight of herself in Lazlo's arms in the huge looking glass above the fire.

We do look beautiful together, she thought dreamily, but something is wrong.

'Would you mind terribly if I went back to being blonde again?' she said.

THE END

RIDERS by JILLY COOPER

'Sex and horses: who could ask for more?'
Sunday Telegraph

If you thought you knew what to expect of Jilly Cooper – bursts of restless romance, strings of domestic disasters, flip fun with the class system – RIDERS will come as a pleasurable surprise.

A multi-stranded love story, it tells of the lives of a tight circle of star riders who move from show to show, united by raging ambition, bitter rivalry and the terror of failure. The superheroes are Jake Lovell, a half-gypsy orphan who wears gold earrings, handles a horse – or a woman – with effortless skill, and is consumed with hatred for the promiscuous upper-class cad, Rupert Campbell-Black, who has no intention of being faithful to his wife, Helen, but is outraged when she runs away with another rider.

'Blockbusting fiction at its best'
David Hughes, The Mail On Sunday

'I defy anyone not to enjoy her book. It is a delight from start to finish'
Auberon Waugh, Daily Mail

0 552 12486 9

RIVALS by JILLY COOPER

'Written with an unflagging energy, it is sexy, stylish and totally riveting'
Options

'Romping along at breathtaking speed, RIVALS is guaranteed to make it'
Today

Jilly Cooper's effervescent new novel explores the cut-throat world of television and lets loose the insatiable libido of the devastatingly attractive hero of RIDERS, Rupert Campbell-Black.

'I couldn't put it down'
Sunday Express

'Jilly Cooper spins a yarn like a speed-loom with pace and verve'
The Times

0 552 13264 0

HARRIET by JILLY COOPER

Shy, dreamy and incurably romantic, Harriet Poole was shattered when her brief affair with Simon Villiers, Oxford's leading playboy undergraduate, ended abruptly, leaving her penniless, alone and pregnant. Still hopelessly in love with Simon, she took baby William and buried herself in deepest Yorkshire as nanny to the children of Cory Erskine, a somewhat eccentric scriptwriter. In that unorthodox household, Harriet felt herself beginning to thaw a little – she grew to love the children, and Cory himself, still infatuated with his estranged wife Noel, came to depend on her in a comfortable kind of way. Local tongues were just beginning to wag when a whole host of visitors began to arrive to disrupt Harriet's peaceful routine: first Noel, hellbent on winning Cory back, then Cory's glamorous brother Kit, whose old affair with Noel didn't stop him making passes at Harriet, and finally, of all people – Simon . . .

0 552 10576 7

OCTAVIA by JILLY COOPER

As soon as Octavia caught a glimpse of Jeremy in the night club, she knew she just had to have him. It didn't matter that he'd just got engaged to an old school friend of hers, plump, good natured Gussie; he was looking at Octavia in the way that suggested bed rather than breakfast, and she was weak at the knees . . . But Octavia was used to men falling in love with her at a moment's notice – it happened all the time if you were rich and as stunning as she was. An invitation to join Gussie and Jeremy for a cosy weekend on a canal barge came like a gift from the gods: How could she fail to hook Jeremy? But the other part of the foursome was whizz-kid business tycoon Gareth Llewellyn, a swarthy Welshman with all the tenderness of a scrum-half . . . definitely not Octavia's type! And one way and another, he certainly managed to thwart her plans . . .

0 552 10717 4

PRUDENCE by JILLY COOPER

The trouble with the Mulholland family, Prudence decided, was that they were all in love with the wrong people. She'd been overjoyed when Pendle, her super-cool barrister boyfriend, invited her home for the weekend to meet his family. At least she might get some reaction out of him – so far he hadn't so much as made a pass at her, after the first night when he'd nearly raped her. But home turned out to be a decaying mansion in the Lake District, and his family included his glamorous, scatty mother who forgot the mounting bills by throwing wild parties, brothers Ace, dark and forbidding, and Jack, handsome, married and only too ready to take over with Pru if Pendle didn't get a move on. It was only when she noticed the way Pendle looked at Jack's wife Maggie that it began to dawn on Pru that there was more to this weekend than met the eye. It looked like a non-stop game of changing partners . . .

0 552 10878 2

IMOGEN by JILLY COOPER

As a librarian, Imogen read a lot of books, but none of them covered Real Life on The Riviera. Her holiday with tennis ace, Nicky, and the whole glamorous coterie of journalist, playboy, photographer, was a revelation – and so was she. A prize worth winning. A wild Yorkshire rose among the thorny model girls, Cable and Yvonne, with a rare asset that they'd mislaid years ago . . . But the path of a jet-set virgin in that lovely wicked world was a hard one. Imogen began to wonder if virtue really was its own reward . . .

0 552 11149 X

EMILY by JILLY COOPER

If Emily hadn't gone to Annie Richmond's party, she would never have met the impossible, irresistible Rory Balniel – never have married him and been carried off to the wild Scottish island of Irasa to live in his ancestral home along with his eccentric mother Coco, and the dog, Walter Scott. She'd never have met the wild and mysterious Marina, a wraith from Rory's past, nor her brother, the disagreeable Finn Maclean; never have spent a night in a haunted highland castle, or been caught stealing roses in a see-through nightie . . . Yes, it all started at Annie Richmond's party . . .

0 552 10277 6

LISA & CO. by JILLY COOPER

Here is a book of love stories of great variety and undoubted class from an author who has endeared herself to millions of readers and who has satisfied them all.

As well as Lisa, we meet Hester, Julia, Helen and Caroline, and a host of other lovely ladies, falling in and out of love, finding, losing (and often finding again) the men of their dreams. LISA & CO. is a celebration of the kind of love story that only Jilly Cooper can write.

0 552 12041 3